# Breaking the Peyote Circle

## A Fernando Lopez Santa Fe Mystery

# Breaking the Peyote Circle

## A Fernando Lopez Santa Fe Mystery

# James C. Wilson

SUNSTONE
PRESS

SANTA FE

Sunstone books may be purchased for educational, business, or sales promotional use.
For information please write: Special Markets Department, Sunstone Press,
P.O. Box 2321, Santa Fe, New Mexico 87504-2321.
Printed on acid-free paper
∞
eBook: 978-1-61139-767-3

**WWW.SUNSTONEPRESS.COM**
SUNSTONE PRESS / POST OFFICE BOX 2321 / SANTA FE, NM 87504-2321 /USA
(505) 988-4418

"Your nightmares follow you like a shadow, forever."
—Aleksandar Hemon, *The Lazarus Project*

# FLASHBACK

First there was a blinding flash of pain in the back of his head. Then his vision cracked and the scene before him crumbled into fragments.

One second he was sitting at the fire circle chanting with the other group members in Apache Canyon, the next he was with his Marine division driving toward Fallujah in Iraq, Sergeant Antonio Blake, 1st Division. He was in the Jeep's passenger seat, lieutenant Murphy at the wheel, as they entered the smoking remains of a mud village of tumbledown houses. Barking dogs and children playing in the dirt among broken walls greeted them. Smoke was closing in from all sides, smothering them.

Thok! Thok! Thok! erupted from somewhere in the village pinging against the side of the jeep. The lieutenant hit the gas.

"Over by the well," someone in the convoy behind them shouted. In response, a hail of bullets ripped through every living thing and building near the well. The shooter, a young boy, burst into fragments of tissue and blood.

Now out of control, the jeep plunged forward. Antonio struggled to open his door, trying to get out. The jeep careened to the right and crashed into an adobe wall. When they hit, the lieutenant pitched sideways into Antonio's lap, trapping him against the door. The lieutenant's head flopped to the side, a bloody tear in his neck gushing blood. Antonio panicked. He tried to stop it with his left hand. Soon he was covered in blood. Cursing, he smashed his nearly 300-pound body against his door and popped it open. They fell into the dust, bodies entwined, legs and arms and torso doused in blood. Antonio screamed.

Thok! Thok! came from a building across the street. Someone else was shooting at them from behind a white mud wall in front of the building.

Antonio kicked out and rolled free of Murphy's body. Feeling dizzy, his vision blurry, he scrambled to his feet and charged the wall. He saw the shooter, a tiny figure wearing street clothes. Antonio stumbled into the ditch on the far side of the road and fell to his knees. The scene in front of him was bleached white by the intense sun. By the time he made it to the wall, the shooter had finished reloading and was raising his assault rifle over the wall. Too late.

Antonio knocked the gun out of the shooter's hands and grabbed him around the neck. Squeezing hard, Antonio picked up the shooter and shook him over and over. He began to hear voices, faint at first and then louder....

"What? Antonio! What have you done?" someone was yelling, pulling on his arms.

The chanting stopped.

Antonio released what he was holding and shook his head, trying to clear his mind. Now he saw the shadowy figures sitting around the flickering campfire, with the hills surrounding Apache Canyon and the Galisteo Creek lost in darkness.

He was back now, back from his deployment in Iraq. No doubt about it, his Post Traumatic Stress Syndrome was getting worse again. He couldn't control the flashbacks and the nightmares. Nothing seemed to work anymore, none of the groups or the therapies he'd tried. Not even crazy Ziggy and his Rancho Nirvana.

"What have you done?" Ziggy said again.

Not understanding, Antonio looked down at the twisted body on the ground at his feet. He recognized the body of Chris Chabot.

What had he done now?

# 1

Fernando Lopez was sitting on the patio of his house on Acequia Madre Street drinking his third cup of coffee when his cell phone rang. He'd forgotten to bring it outside, left it somewhere inside, probably the kitchen. But as soon as he stepped though the kitchen door the ringing stopped. He finally found it on the coffee table in the living room, where he must have left it last night after watching the ten o'clock news. He took it into the kitchen and sat down at the kitchen table.

When he saw the name of Manny Alvarez on the screen, he debated whether to call back or delete the message. Manny had replaced Fernando a few years back as the lead detective at the Santa Fe Police Department. Every time Manny called it meant trouble, usually big trouble. Even though Fernando was no longer a police detective or even a private investigator, Manny and a whole lot of other people in Santa Fe called him to solve their problems. So much so that Fernando had taken to calling himself a 'fixer,' a guy who cleaned up other people's messes, either legally or in that gray area between legal and illegal. Semi-legally? Quasi-legally?

So far he only took cases involving people he knew. Everyone else could clean up their own damn messes.

Sighing, Fernando hit the call back button.

"Fernando. I've been trying to contact you all morning," Manny said.

"Yeah, I've been outside on the patio," Fernando said. "What's up?"

"It's Antonio, he's in big trouble," Manny replied. "Did you know that his Post Traumatic Stress Disorder has come back with a vengeance?"

"No, I haven't heard from Antonio in a few weeks," Fernando said. "I thought he was happy being retired, living out there in the Pecos in the cabin he built. Why would the PTSD come back now?"

"That's the thing," Manny said. "It never completely goes away. It can erupt at any time. Sometimes it's when Antonio gets stressed. Sometimes there doesn't seem to be a reason. He's been having bad dreams and not sleeping, just like before. I've been out there several times over the last two weeks, taking him to appointments at the V.A. and once to Christus Saint Vincent Hospital."

Surprised, Fernando said, "Jesus, I had no idea. I know PTSD ruined his marriage back in the day. Before he moved to Santa Fe."

"Well, I could be wrong, but I wonder if the reappearance of Jack Lacy, Antonio's old war buddy, triggered this latest episode."

Fernando remembered Jack Lacy all too well. Lacy was known to law enforcement as the Santa Fe Assassin. Lacy had served in the same Marine unit with Antonio in the first Iraq war. After his discharge, Lacy had become a professional hit man, using his skills as a highly trained sniper to kill politicians and business types in Eastern Europe and the Mideast for huge sums of money. He arrived in Santa Fe on a contract to kill a high-ranking government official scheduled to appear at Chaco Canyon. When the event had to be cancelled because of a riot, Lacy refused to return a $250,000 advance. In return, his employer had contacted the Sinaloa Cartel to get the advance back one way or another. In the war between Lacy and the Sinaloa Cartel that followed, both Antonio and Fernando were drawn into the bloodshed on the side of Lacy. Not one of their finest days. Something Fernando would like to forget, even though Lacy was victorious in the end. A killing machine.

"That makes sense," Fernando responded. "Jack Lacy gave me nightmares for weeks after he left town. Talk about a cold-blooded killer. I've never seen anyone that scary."

"I know, so it makes sense that Lacy might have brought this on," Manny said. "Antonio's been seeing a doctor at the V.A. for medication. He's so desperate that he's even been going to a quack therapist, a con man who calls himself Doctor Ziggy and who operates a rehab facility out in Apache Canyon by the name of Rancho Nirvana. I kid you not, Rancho Nirvana. Ziggy offers a bunch of far-out therapies there, including hypnosis and peyote ceremonies that supposedly help with PTSD."

"Peyote ceremonies?" Fernando interrupted Manny. He still remembered his peyote wolf case. For years afterward he had nightmares of a wolfman bursting into a teepee during a peyote ceremony.

"I'm afraid so...and during one of these ceremonies Antonio apparently lost it," Manny said. "He had a flashback and choked one of the other patients. At least that's what we're being told."

"So what, you're saying Antonio killed this guy?" Fernando asked, hoping he had misunderstood.

"He's the number one suspect—in fact, the only suspect at the moment," Manny said. "And to make matters worse, the patient he allegedly killed was none other than Chris Chabot, the District Attorney's wayward son."

Shocked, Fernando didn't know what to say. He shook his head and mumbled something under his breath that he was glad he didn't say out loud. Manny was only doing his job.

"What the hell is Chris Chabot doing at a peyote ceremony?" Fernando asked, finding it difficult to believe that the District Attorney's son was gobbling peyote at Rancho Nirvana.

"Well, Chris has been fighting addiction all his adult life," Manny said. "Plus he has a host of financial and personal problems. In short, he's a mess."

"Well, let's don't get ahead of ourselves," Fernando said, sighing. "Where's Antonio now?"

"Good question, that's why I'm calling," Manny said. "We can't find him. We went out to his cabin twice yesterday with a warrant, but he wasn't there. Neither was his Jeep Wrangler. Looks like he's fled."

"Have you tried calling him?" Fernando asked.

"Doesn't ring. He must have turned off his cell phone or tossed it," Manny replied.

Fernando leaned back in his kitchen chair, trying to relax. He felt a wave of anxiety sweep over him. Antonio?

"Are you still there?" Manny asked.

"Yeah...so what do you want me to do?" Fernando answered.

Manny laughed. "Find Antonio. And when you do, tell him to lawyer up, because he's going to need a good one to get him out of this mess."

"I'll tell him to call Raoul Garcia," Fernando said. Raoul, though not in the best of health, was the best defense lawyer in the state of New Mexico, hands down.

"Good idea," Manny said. "If anyone can get him off, Raoul can."

With that, Manny clicked off, leaving Fernando holding a silent phone.

## 2

Fernando hadn't told Manny or any of his other friends that he'd been having his own recurring nightmares. Only his wife Estelle knew, having to wake him when he started screaming or thrashing around in their bed. Lately his nightmares had been about Jack Lacy, the so-called Santa Fe assassin. In his nightmare this morning Fernando was standing in the parking lot of the old Forest Service building on Upper Canyon Road no more than twenty feet from Silva Archivada, the head of the Sinaloa Cartel in the Southwest, when Lacy fired his high-powered sniper rifle from the hillside. First the crack! and then the top of Lacy's head exploded. Blood and tissue flying everywhere. Then he turned and saw Lacy's sniper rifle move to the side and point directly at him! He woke up screaming, his legs churning under the sheets as he tried to run away, out of Lacy's range.

"Wake up! Wake up!" Estelle said, shaking him by the shoulders until he stopped screaming and lay still. She blamed his refusal to completely retire for his nightmares. "I don't know what you call yourself now, a private investigator, a fixer, a witch doctor, whatever, but you have to stop! You understand? Stop!"

He knew she was right, but he kept getting drawn back into danger by friends and acquaintances who needed help extricating themselves from messy situations. Now Antonio needed his help, one of his oldest friends. Not only that, but Antonio had saved his ass on more occasions than he could count during the years they both worked at the Santa Fe Police Department, Antonio as a sergeant and him as lead detective. No question about it, he had to get involved.

Fernando had no choice. Question was: where to begin. He decided to first pay a visit to Antonio's cabin in the Pecos and then to Ziggy's Rancho Nirvana in Apache Canyon, both of them on the same highway.

So after deciding he wouldn't need his Smith & Wesson, he locked up the house and climbed into his Cherokee. Then he drove down Acequia Madre to the Paseo and turned left. He followed the Paseo to Old Santa Fe Trail and turned left again enjoying the small quaint adobes with their brightly painted blue doors and windowsills, surrounded by yellow sunflowers and red hollyhocks.

Eventually Old Santa Fe Trail fed into the Old Las Vegas Highway, with the Santa Fe National Forest and the green foothills of the Sangre de Cristo Mountains off to his left. He passed by the exit to Apache Canyon and continued on toward the town of Pecos.

About a mile from Pecos Fernando turned north on the county road that led to Antonio's cabin. Antonio's dirt driveway was a mile up the county road. The Cherokee bounced over the rough drive, forcing Fernando to slow down approaching the cabin. Built under a stand of tall ponderosa pines, the cabin sat at the edge of the national forest, which extended all the way back to the Santa Fe Ski Basin. A beautiful location, but too damn remote for Fernando's taste. He knew the location had been therapeutic for Antonio, who had moved here after a severe bout of Post Traumatic Stress Disorder had ruined his marriage. He'd been a loner ever since, enjoying the isolation of living in the wild Pecos Wilderness.

Fernando pulled up under the ponderosa pines and switched off the big engine. Antonio's Jeep Wrangler was missing, just as Manny had reported. He climbed out of the Cherokee and walked to the door of the cabin. Antonio had built the cabin himself from a log kit he'd bought in Colorado. Very primitive, with no running water or electricity, the cabin had a heavy steel door and windows for security, which is the one thing Antonio wanted, privacy.

Fernando was surprised to find the front door unlocked, so he helped himself and stepped into the one-room cabin. Looked pretty much the same as Fernando remembered it: messy and cluttered with discarded newspapers, empty beer cans, and dirty dishes on the slab of particle board Antonio used as a kitchen counter. On the counter sat a water basin and the REI cooler Antonio used as a refrigerator. A wood stove, which Antonio used for cooking and for heat during the winter months, occupied one corner of the cabin, next to a pile of wood on the slat floor.

Looking around, Fernando noticed Antonio's sleeping bag was missing from the army surplus cot along the rear wall, which served as Antonio's bedroom. So, too, was the canvas duffle bag Antonio used as a suitcase whenever he travelled. Antonio kept the duffle shoved between his cot and an old mahogany dresser he'd found in an antique store and used to store his clothes, instead of a closet. Apparently Antonio had fled in his Wrangler, taking with him his sleeping bag and whatever clothing he could stuff into his duffle bag.

Did not look good for Antonio. That was all Fernando thought about as he stepped out of the cabin and closed the steel door behind him. Instead of staying to clear his name, the big man had fled. Or so it seemed.

The fact that Antonio had run only made his situation worse. Innocent people didn't run. That was the theory,

Manny would have an APB out shortly, if he hadn't sent it out already. It wouldn't take long before someone spotted a new model Jeep Wrangler driven by a six-foot, eight-inch, two-hundred-eighty-pound man. Spotting him would be one thing, bringing him in would be another. Known as the enforcer back in his days at the Washington Avenue Station, Antonio was not only enormous but strong as an ox. Even worse, he had a nasty temper, not to mention a short fuse, thanks to Post Traumatic Stress Disorder.

Fernando leaned against his Cherokee, trying to think where Antonio might be headed. The big man didn't have many friends other than Fernando and Manny. He'd been a loner for years, living out here in his cabin.

With no leads and no plan, Fernando decided to bite the bullet and head for Ziggy's Rancho Nirvana, a place he'd been trying to avoid for a couple of reasons, first and foremost because Ziggy was bat-shit crazy.

# 3

Doctor Ziggy, aka Frank Tate, wasn't really a doctor. An ex-rockabilly musician and Ken Kesey wannabe who drove an old school bus painted psychedelic colors, Tate resurfaced a few years back claiming to hold an online certificate in substance abuse counseling from some fly-by-night institution in the Midwest. He set up shop at what was left of an old ranch in Apache Canyon, calling himself Doctor Ziggy after the reggae music he blared constantly from his ranch house. His years as a bartender had made him a good listener, so he created various therapy groups to counsel those afflicted by drugs, alcohol, violence, and different forms of anxiety. His unorthodox methods, most involving illegal drugs, were ridiculed by board-certified psychiatrists and psychologists but praised by his former patients who claimed to have been 'cured' by Ziggy, whose exuberance and magnetic personality always won their support.

In other words, Ziggy was a fast-talking confidence man and a would-be guru who had been able to bamboozle his followers and those health department officials who allowed him to continue offering his strange brand of counseling out in Apache Canyon. It helped that Apache Canyon was seen as a kind of no-man's land east of Santa Fe, southeast of Eldorado, and west of Pecos, where jurisdiction was either indeterminate or non-existent, depending on who you asked.

Back when he was a private investigator Fernando had the misfortune of dealing with Ziggy. A mother had come to Fernando claiming her son had been kidnapped and drugged by the leader of a cult out in Apache Canyon, namely Ziggy. Fernando managed to find the woman's son at Rancho Nirvana where he was being treated for anxiety, but the kid was so drugged out on psilocybin, LSD, and good old marijuana that he could barely talk. When the kid committed suicide later, the Santa Fe Police Department tried to pin a murder rap on Tate. In response, Ziggy hired Raoul Garcia, the best defense lawyer in the state, who hadn't lost a case in years. Raoul totally changed the narrative by arguing that the kid's suicide resulted not from a reaction to drugs provided to him at Rancho Nirvana but from years of sexual abuse by the kid's father, who happened to be deceased and unable to offer much of a defense. The jury sided with Raoul. As it always did.

The case left a bad taste in Fernando's mouth. When Ziggy walked free, he vowed never to set foot on Rancho Nirvana again. But here he was, like it or not, driving back down the Old Las Vegas Highway looking for the road into Apache Canyon. He recognized the turn-off when he spotted the small Cañoncito Church, white with a tiny red bell tower on top.

Fernando turned left and followed the winding blacktop into the canyon. When the road forked, he turned right and drove the Cherokee up the hillside to Rancho Nirvana, a tumbledown collection of wood frame buildings and an old abandoned school bus painted in bright psychedelic colors and images, a leftover from Ziggy's counterculture years.

Fernando pulled into the gravel parking lot and surveyed the property. He saw several run-down casitas, formerly bunk houses, each with its own outhouse. The office and main house where Ziggy lived was on a hill above the parking lot, connected by a flagstone stairway that zig-zagged up the hill. Other buildings included a shed, a small dilapidated barn with a collapsed roof, and what looked like a pump house. Same as Fernando remembered it, except for the people. Where was everyone? Looked like the place was deserted. Last time he was here there were at least a dozen people drugged out of their minds and roaming half naked around the canyon.

Climbing out of his Cherokee, Fernando walked up the flagstone path to the main house, which had a long veranda in front and a pitched roof cluttered with chimneys and weather vanes. Looked like something out of an Alfred Hitchcock horror movie, which seemed out of place, given its supposedly therapeutic purpose. He didn't see Ziggy until he started walking up the wooden steps to the veranda. Ziggy was reclining in an old rocking chair with his cowboy boots resting on the porch railing, eyes closed.

"Tate...are you dead?" Fernando asked.

"Hell no, I'm meditating," Ziggy said, opening his eyes. "I heard you drive up. I knew you were coming. Man, I know everything about you, Lopez. I'm a seer, in case you've forgotten. And I no longer abide by the moniker of Tate. Call me by my professional name, Ziggy."

Fernando laughed. "Professional? Sounds like the name of someone who escaped from the Las Vegas loony bin."

Ziggy frowned and pounded his chest. "Now that hurts."

"Where is everyone?" Fernando asked, still looking around the canyon for the usual crowd.

Ziggy shook his head and stood up, a short slender man with long curly hair down to his shoulders and a handlebar mustache, once blond but now streaked with gray. His face was the color of saddle leather, matching the leather vest he wore over a tie-dyed T-shirt and faded blue jeans. He looked like a poor man's version of Buffalo Bill, the famous cowboy showman. Either that or a carnival barker with a touch of Ken Kesey, the Acid King.

"Long gone, my friend," Ziggy said, shaking his head sadly. "I've only been doing outpatient therapy for the last year or so. Too many hassles with the man. Once in a while I make an exception for someone who needs immediate help...intense help. Like your friend Antonio. That's why you're here, right?"

Fernando nodded. "So what happened?"

Ziggy pointed to the outbuildings. "I put him up in that first bunk house after he showed up with a bad case of Post Traumatic Stress Disorder. He was a haunted man. Couldn't sleep because of nightmares. Man, he even had flashbacks during the day that would send him off the deep end into a terrible rage. I thought he might hurt himself or someone else, so I kept him here, where I could keep an eye on him. Didn't help, though. I did my best, but some people you just can't fix. They're too far gone. Surely you've experienced the same thing in your profession—or professions. What do you call yourself now, a private investigator?"

"I call myself a fixer," Fernando replied.

"Well, you must be a magic man if you can fix people on demand, just like that. Would that it were that easy," Ziggy lamented.

"I'm still waiting to hear what happened to Antonio," Fernando said.

"Fair enough, then follow me," Ziggy said, motioning for Fernando to follow him inside.

Fernando followed Ziggy into a large front room that he vaguely remembered, with a wooden plank floor and bare, rough-cut pine walls without paint or wallpaper of any kind. Instead, Tate had hung several Buddhist posters on the walls with names like 'Buddhist Mindfulness,' 'Mandala of the Medicine Buddha,' 'Buddhist Wheel of Life,' and 'The Seven Virtues of Bushido.' The room contained four rows of old church pews Ziggy had salvaged from some abandoned church. The pews faced a podium, where Ziggy apparently preached and blathered his sermon. Behind the podium stood a large white board where Tate had written a quote from a psychiatry research paper and its citation:

"Nightmares may be a common clinical characteristic for people experiencing psychotic symptoms. Further, the distress associated with them is associated with worse daytime symptoms. These results support the assertion ... that nightmares should be considered as a separate problem that can be comorbid with a range of other diagnoses, including BPD, primary insomnia, PTSD, and now psychosis."

The source was listed below in small print:

"Nightmares in Patients with Psychosis: The Relation with Sleep, Psychotic, Affective, and Cognitive Symptoms," B. Sheaves, *et al.* *Canadian Journal of Psychiatry*, August, 2015 p.354-361.

Fernando studied the citation for a moment and then asked, "So you actually read research in this area then?"

"But of course," Ziggy said. "I'm licensed."

Licensed in what, Tate didn't say.

"What is BPD?" Fernando asked.

"Bipolar Disorder, of course," Ziggy said. "What else could it be?"

Fernando ignored Ziggy.

"This way," Ziggy said, taking Fernando straight into a rear sitting room, equipped with wooden chairs and a beat-up sofa. Outside a pair of tall windows Fernando saw a fire circle, the thing he remembered most about Rancho Nirvana. Tate held his peyote ceremonies in the fire circle, a collection of beat-up wooden chairs and benches arranged around a fire pit. Staring into the fire, the attendees would gobble peyote and supposedly talk about their problems while hallucinating and having visions. Therapeutic? Fernando had to wonder.

In fact, Fernando had to wonder about a lot of things. Like why give a hallucinogenic to people who are suffering from anxiety? Are the visions and hallucinations supposed to make them less anxious? From his albeit limited experience dropping acid back in the day, the weird stuff he saw while hallucinating for damned sure didn't make him less anxious or more relaxed. No, the stuff he remembered seeing scared the hell out of him.

"Antonio was sitting right here, at my side," Ziggy said, standing over the wooden bench closest to the house. "I had three other people in the circle that night, in addition to Chris Chabot, who was siting directly across from Antonio. We started about eight o'clock, each of them eating a button of peyote and taking the sacrament. Eventually they started talking about themselves and whatever they were seeing or imagining. Then about ten o'clock, right after the first scheduled Water Call, Antonio started moaning and rocking back and forth. Then he started screaming."

"Screaming what?" Fernando asked.

Ziggy shrugged. "Crazy stuff, man. I couldn't make it out. He just lost it completely. Before I could calm him down, he ran across to Chris Chabot and grabbed Chris by the neck and shook him like a rag doll. By the time I got over there and managed to pry his hands off Chris' neck, Chris was already dead. Nothing I could do but call the cops. Lord knows I didn't want to call them, but what choice did I have? Another dead man on my ranch? I knew the pigs would nail me for something. I remember the last time that happened."

Fernando listened to Ziggy's version of events and then shook his head. "I don't understand. Why would you ever give peyote to someone suffering from anxiety and PTSD?"

"Man, there's nothing better for anxiety," Ziggy said. "It's much better than acid, even weed, which just makes you drowsy. I use peyote all the time. Here-" he said, reaching into his pocket for a small plastic bag. He took out one wrinkled brown button of peyote and handed it to Fernando. "Try it. It will open the doors of perception, just like Huxley said."

"Yeah, I've heard it all before, but will it bring relief to someone suffering from anxiety or PTSD?" Fernando asked, not convinced.

"Hell, yes it will," Ziggy said. "You're not listening to me, Lopez. The peyote rite is one of prayer and quiet contemplation. Trust me, nothing's better for anxiety, because the rite incorporates a powerful mechanism for the liquidation of individual anxieties. I'm talking about the practice of public confession...of sins. If someone's struggling with a bad memory or something he regrets in his past, he might experience a vivid revelation in which he sees or hears the spirits of those involved and be shown the way to resolve the lingering wound starting with a public confession, seeking repentance before the group. Fact is, through peyote you acquire increased powers of concentration and introspection, so much so that it becomes a religious experience. All that and it's not even habit-forming."

"You sound like a goddamn snake oil salesman," Fernando said.

Ziggy smiled broadly.

Fernando bit his tongue. Why waste his time arguing with a certified con man? He deposited the peyote button in his shirt pocket. Then he took a notebook out of his rear pocket and handed it to Ziggy. "Write down the names of the other three people who were here."

Ziggy wrote down the three names and handed back the notebook.

"Antonio's really suffering, man," Ziggy said. "He needs your help. You have to find him before he does something drastic."

Fernando sighed. "I'm trying."

## 4

Fernando sat in his Cherokee holding the brown button in the palm of his hand. He knew peyote came from a small, blue cactus that grew wild in parts of southern Texas and Mexico. The cactus produced white flowers, as well as mushroom-like crowns that contained mescaline, a naturally occurring psychedelic drug that produced vivid hallucinations and deep introspection and finally nausea. Members of the Native American Church prized the dried crowns and used them in their all-night peyote meetings.

He knew from personal experience, and from questioning people involved in his peyote wolf case, that when chewed peyote induces extraordinary physiological and psychological effects such as bright colors and visions. It was as though you were witnessing not a vision but a real, ongoing scene you were completely aware of your actual environment and in possession of all your mental faculties, or so you thought. These shifts in time and perception created a bifurcation of reality, so to speak.

Some people argued that peyote unlocked the door to a separate, higher reality. Whatever that meant. He'd always been dubious when anyone talked to him about a 'higher reality.' To him it was just bullshit that con artists like Ziggy used to bilk their needy clients, all of them desperate to find cures for their physical and spiritual ailments. That was his considered opinion anyway.

Fernando had his own experiences with peyote, both personal and professional. He'd made the mistake of eating a couple of buttons one fourth of July afternoon at Cañjilon Lakes back when he was a teenager. It seemed like a million years ago–1978, or maybe 1979. The Lopez family had gone up to Cañjilon for a reunion, a weekend of camping and fishing. His cousin Manuel, who was a member of the Native American Church, brought a bag of peyote and shared it with him and some of the older cousins at Cañjilon.

After the peyote took effect, he wandered off by himself to lie in the grass and watch the sky change colors like a giant kaleidoscope. He didn't remember how long he laid there, only the feeling of being incapacitated, unable to move. Personally, he didn't care much for the feeling, or for the sense of powerlessness he experienced while under the influence of the drug. The loss of control frightened him. That was the higher reality he found: helplessness.

His peyote wolf case brought that experience back to him. For months afterward he had nightmares of a wolfman bursting into a teepee during a peyote ceremony. Scared the hell out of him. Until finally he decided the recurring dream was offering him a way of understanding his fear of the unknown, the darkness at the heart of human experience. What we did not know and would never know but somehow managed to live with every moment of every day. Something like that.

So here he was, sitting in his Cherokee in Apache Canyon, waiting for direction or inspiration that would lead him to the right path. He closed his eyes and tried to picture the murder, Antonio rushing across the fire circle and grabbing Chris Chabot by the neck...but it took a long time to choke someone to death, it wasn't quick...so why wouldn't Tate or someone else try to intervene? Or did they?

When he opened his eyes Fernando had a plan. First he would pay a visit to the Santa Fe Police Forensics office at Christus Saint Vincent Hospital. He wanted to know more about Chabot's wounds. He would start there and then round up the other three witnesses to get their accounts of what happened to Chabot.

With that in mind, he drove back to the Old Las Vegas Highway and followed it into Santa Fe, turning left on what became Saint Michael's Drive. He pulled into the hospital parking lot and found a spot near the main entrance. He climbed out of the Cherokee and walked into the hospital, taking an elevator down to the basement. Forensics was at the end of the long hallway, cold and windowless. Made him uncomfortable every time he set foot in here.

When Fernando walked through the automatic door he found Miguel standing at the counter. Teresa, the other long-time Forensic worker, was nowhere in sight.

"Fernando... long time, no see," Miguel said.

"Yeah, I'm pretty much retired," Fernando replied. "These days I only take a few cases."

"What can I do for you?"

"I'm looking for information about Chris Chabot, the guy who was strangled out in Apache Canyon the other day," Fernando said. "Is the body still here?"

Miguel shook his head. "No, we sent it down to the Medical Examiner in Albuquerque. We're not sure about the cause of death."

That surprised Fernando. Manny and Ziggy made it sound cut and dried that Antonio had choked Chris Chabot. "What do you mean?"

"Well, we know the guy was strangled, but not exactly how," Miguel said. "We did find finger marks and bruises around his neck, but we also found a circular indentation line around his neck that may or may not have been caused by the tight bolo tie he was wearing. Even more confusing, we found a second, smaller circular indentation line around the guy's neck. Looks like this one might have been caused by a wire garrote. Anyway, that's why we wanted the Medical Examiner to look at the body. They have better resources than we do."

"No kidding," Fernando said, mostly to himself. That changed everything. Antonio may have grabbed Chris Chabot by the neck, but someone else may have choked Chabot to death with a wire garrote. Or maybe the bolo tie?

"Do you think a bolo tie tightened around someone's neck could kill a person?" Fernando asked.

Miguel shook his head. "I wouldn't think so, but what do I know?"

Fernando laughed. "Aren't you supposed to be the expert?"

They laughed together and decided what they did know was a drop in the bucket compared to what they didn't know. And would ever know.

Leaving Christus Saint Vincent Hospital always made Fernando feel great: he could walk out of the hospital on his own two feet because he was still alive. Alive! It was a fucking privilege to be alive, even though most people didn't seem to understand that.

For lack of anything better to do, he decided to visit his friend and former landlord Ruby Montez, who'd let him use the garage of her gallery as an office back when he was a private investigator. Now that he was a fixer, he worked from home. He wanted to keep his work on the down-low, keep out of the public eye, so to speak. The people who needed him would find him.

So he backtracked to Old Pecos Trail/Old Santa Fe Trail and took it downtown. He turned right on the Paseo and again on Canyon Road, driving up through the shops and galleries that lined the street, the artistic center of Santa Fe. He turned left into his former parking lot, wedged between Ruby's gallery, The Three Cities of Spain, and Essentia, the sex shop. The building he used as an office sat back between the two buildings, idle now.

Fernando parked beside Ruby's Honda Accord. He set the brake and climbed out of his Cherokee, walking up to the porch of Ruby's gallery. A bell rang loudly as he opened the door and stepped inside.

"Hey Fernando," Ruby said, coming out of the small room she called the lunch room in the back of the gallery. Looked like she'd just come from her pottery co-op in the Railyard District, which she ran with a number of other potters, mostly women. Her jeans and navy blue halter top were both smudged with gray clay. In spite of the clay she remained, as always, gorgeous with her long black hair lightly streaked with gray and her black, bedroom eyes.

He and Ruby went back a long way, even before he met and married Estelle. Always prickly, Ruby wore her bad attitude with pride. To her, it was a badge of honor. Her in-your-face personality put off many people but had made her a force in Santa Fe politics for over two decades. A potter by trade, Ruby had risen through the ranks of *La Raza* to become the most progressive member of City Council ever. Back in the 1990s she fought tooth and nail against all the greedy developers who wanted to turn downtown Santa Fe into one big shopping mall. She led rallies, marches, protests, sit-ins, and if you believed the rumors, a fire-bombing or two.

She lost, of course. The tide of gentrification sweeping over Santa Fe during those years hollowed out the city. Gone were most of the people whose families had lived in Santa Fe for generations. Increasingly higher home values and property taxes priced out all who couldn't afford the million-dollar homes. After two tumultuous terms on City Council lecturing, berating, cajoling, and threatening the other members, she said 'fuck it' and retired to her pottery co-op.

Still she refused to be silenced. She made it a point to attend most Council meetings and give the members a piece of her mind. Every one of them feared Ruby's tirades. Occasionally her anger would get the better of her language and she would be asked to leave. Once a few years back City Council banned her for a year, but her lawyer, Raoul Garcia, sued their asses and got her reinstated in her front row seat staring down the Council.

Over the years he and Ruby had always been friendly, probably because they felt the same way about gentrification and Santa Fe politics in general. That is, they usually ended up on the losing side. So it goes.

"You want the key to your old office back?" Ruby asked. "I'm still hoping you'll change your mind."

Fernando laughed. "No, I'm working from home now that I'm retired. Sort of retired."

"You keep saying you're retired—I'll believe it when I see it," Ruby said. "Come on back to the lunch room, I'll make some coffee."

Fernando followed her back to the lunch room, where Ruby had installed a counter top, a mini fridge, a microwave, and a Keurig coffee maker. She popped a pod into the Keurig and brewed him a cup of coffee and then brewed one for herself.

"So what's new?" Ruby asked, sipping her black coffee.

Fernando frowned. "This hasn't been in the papers yet, I don't think, but have you heard about Antonio and Chris Chabot?"

Ruby shook her head.

Fernando dumped milk and sugar in his coffee cup and then repeated what Manny had told him about Antonio's Post Traumatic Stress Syndrome and what had happened at Rancho Nirvana with Chris Chabot. That Antonio was now the chief suspect in Chabot's murder.

"Wait...are you saying that Manny actually thinks Antonio strangled Chris Chabot?"

"He's the primary suspect," Fernando said. "And to make matters worse, he's disappeared. He must have taken off, maybe gone into hiding somewhere. We've checked his cabin in the Pecos, but his Jeep Wrangler hasn't been there since the murder."

Ruby shook her head. "Jesus! What are you planning to do?"

"Well, I need to find him, for starters," Fernando said. "After that, I don't know what I'll do."

Ruby clucked her tongue but said nothing.

"What do you know about Chris Chabot? Other than he's the son of the district attorney?" Fernando asked, since Ruby seemed to know virtually everyone in Santa Fe. She also kept up with all the gossip in town.

"Hah! He's the black sheep of the family," Ruby said. "He's been in and out of rehab for years because of a Fentanyl addiction. Steve takes him out of state, to facilities in Denver or Phoenix trying to keep his problems hidden, but I think everyone knows by now."

"Well, I for one didn't know," Fernando interrupted. "Chabot and I have never gotten along."

"As far as I know Chris has never been able to hold down a job," Ruby continued. "His father kicked him out of the house but still pays his rent at Fort Marcy Apartments. In other words, he still lives off his father."

Fernando nodded "I guess that explains what he was doing at Rancho Nirvana."

Ruby nodded. "So let me get this straight, Manny says Antonio strangled Chris while having a recurrence of his PTSD?"

"Yes...and so did Frank Tate, or Doctor Ziggy as he calls himself these days," Fernando replied.

Ruby laughed at the mention of Doctor Ziggy. "Yeah, well, Frank Tate is fucking crazy. He's even worse than Chris. I've known him for years, back when he was driving a psychedelic school bus up and down Canyon Road playing guru and picking up young women, most of them underage. Even after that, when he hooked up with an equally crazy woman named Lulu, who he married. Their marriage didn't last long, though. I think Lulu disappeared after a year or two. Since then Tate's been addicted to every substance you can name. I don't know how he keeps going. He should have OD'd years ago."

"He's still playing the guru, except now it's with peyote ceremonies," Fernando said.

Ruby shook her head sadly. "You see what I mean? How's peyote supposed to help Post Traumatic Stress Disorder? Eating peyote causes visions and psychic dislocations that are exactly like PTSD. How do you cure psychic dislocations by giving someone more psychic dislocations?"

Fernando nodded. "I agree."

"No, Frank Tate is fucking crazy," Ruby said. "Always has been."

# 5

Fernando found himself trapped in a dark house trying to find his way out. The floorboards creaked as he shuffled over the wooden floor. Somewhere in the house he heard a woman weeping softly in the darkness. If he could only find her, maybe he could do something to help her, but he kept bumping against walls and pieces of furniture. As his eyes began to adjust, he could make out hulking shadows in the darkness, objects that he tried to avoid as he moved ahead one step at a time. He heard the weeping grow louder as he crept further into the house of darkness.

"Fernando...wake up!" his wife Estelle said, shaking him by the shoulder. When he opened his eyes he saw Estelle standing beside their bed fully dressed, ready to leave for work at the Saint Francis Immigrant Outreach Program, a church nonprofit that helped provide food and clothing to the growing immigrant community in Santa Fe, a sanctuary city.

"Here, Antonio just texted," she said, handing him his cell phone. "Didn't you say he was missing? I'm leaving for work now."

Fernando mumbled something and grabbed the cell phone. He'd told her last night about Antonio and what had happened at Rancho Nirvana. He looked at the screen: "Hang tight, I'll be in touch."

No location. Not much to go on. Where the hell was he?

"Be back around five," Estelle said, walking out the door of their bedroom.

Fernando waved and then sat up in bed. These days he tended to wake up groggy, so he sat there for a few minutes clearing his mind of the dreams and nightmares he'd been having the last few months, most relating to bad memories from his years as a Santa Fe Police detective and a private investigator. Now this dream of being trapped in a dark house. Even during his waking hours he found himself suddenly going to the dark place, reliving moments of danger and violence that he wanted desperately to forget. Easier said than done. So much guilt, so many things he regretted, things he should have done differently or not at all. A never-ending reel of bad juju.

Eventually he went into the bathroom to do his business, taking care to avoid looking in the mirror. One of his superstitions. He was convinced that he aged every time he looked in a mirror, so if only he didn't look in this or any other mirror he wouldn't age. Ever.

After he cleaned up and dressed, he shuffled down to the kitchen and poured himself a cup of coffee from the pot Estelle had made. Then he took his coffee outside to their patio and sat on his bench thinking about Antonio. Sitting on the patio always managed to cheer him. He and Estelle had bought their sweet little adobe on Acequia Madre Street when they first married, some forty years ago. Their adobe had become something of an eyesore on pricey Acequia Madre, where their neighbors, newcomers mostly, had remodeled and expanded their houses into million-dollar mansions that none of the locals could ever afford.

As soon as he finished his coffee he tried to call Antonio, but the big man's cell phone didn't ring. Antonio probably turned the phone off so he couldn't be traced, Fernando figured. That meant he wouldn't be able to find Antonio until Antonio wanted to be found.

So what to do? He debated paying a visit to Chris Chabot's father Steve, the District Attorney of Santa Fe, but cancelled that idea immediately. He didn't particularly like or get along with Steve, who back in the day when Fernando was a Santa Fe Police detective always gave him and the other cops a hard time. Always wanted more evidence before he would bring charges against the suspects they arrested. Never enough evidence for Steve. Used to drive him crazy.

That left the other three people who were present at the fire circle when and where Chris Chabot was supposedly murdered. He looked at his notebook where Ziggy had jotted down the names of the three attendees: Mary Logan, George Boros, and Tom Lujan. He would start with Mary and work his way down the list. First, though, he needed some breakfast.

Fernando found a cheese enchilada smothered in red chile that survived last night's meal, so he warmed it quickly in the microwave and gobbled it down. Then he went into his study and booted up his laptop. He found a Mary Logan out on Agua Fria Street and dialed the number listed for her.

"Hello, I'm calling Mary Logan," Fernando said.

"Who's calling?" asked the young man who answered the phone. He didn't sound very damn friendly.

"I'm a friend of Doctor Ziggy's," Fernando said. "I just wanted to ask her some questions about the incident the other day at Rancho Nirvana."

Suddenly the line went dead. The young man had hung up on him.

Fernando cursed under his breath and made a note of Mary Logan's address in his notebook, in case he decided to pay an unexpected visit.

Then he moved on to the next name on his list, George Boros. Fortunately Boros himself answered. "Yeah...sure, I can help you out," Boros said, after Fernando introduced himself. "I'm just leaving for a nine o'clock doctor's appointment, but I can meet you downtown, say about ten?"

"Good. How about we meet on the Plaza?"

"I'll be there," Boros said and clicked off.

Fernando took his time before leaving. He tried calling Antonio again but the line remained dead. He decided to postpone contacting Tom Lujan, who happened to be an old acquaintance from his younger days. He knew Tom had gone through periods of addiction and homelessness. Last he heard Tom was living in someone's guest house out in La Cienega.

A few minutes before ten o'clock Fernando locked up the house and drove his Cherokee down to the Paseo and over to Alameda. Out of habit he always parked on Alameda along the Santa Fe River. Sure, he was somewhat OCD, but so what. He had his routines and stuck with them. Routines were his way of bringing order to his life. What else was there?

By the time he walked up Shelby Street to the Plaza it was a few minutes past ten o'clock. Entering the southeast corner of the Plaza on San Francisco Street he spotted a heavy-set man waving at him from over by the Bandstand. Worth a try.

"Howdy Lopez," the man said as Fernando approached. "I recognized you from photos I've seen in the *Independent*."

"Nice to meet you," Fernando said and shook the man's hand.

They sat on the nearest bench. After an awkward moment, Boros asked, "So how can I help you?"

"I'm curious about what happened in the fire circle at Rancho Nirvana the night Chris Chabot died," Fernando said. "You were there, right?"

Boros nodded. "I've been a regular for the past two months, ever since my divorce was finalized and I lost my job. A double whammy. I've been really depressed and anxious, not knowing what to do next. I don't like to be alone. I've been taking anti-depressants—in fact, I just came from the doctor's office to get a refill for my Xanax, which helps with my anxiety. But I've found that eating peyote helps even more than the pills."

"So I've been told," Fernando said. "It doesn't complicate the anxiety or make it worse?"

Boros shook his head. "No."

"So can you tell me what happened that night?" Fernando asked.

"Sure. I came early that day because I wanted to talk to Chris, who'd borrowed money from me a couple of months ago. Now that I had lost my job, I needed him to repay the loan. As usual, he said he didn't have the money. He never had any money because he never worked. He couldn't hold down a job."

"So I understand," Fernando said, interrupting Boros.

"Anyway, we got in an argument over the money he owed me and rather than letting it get out of hand, I went for a walk to cool off. By the time I got back the meeting had already started. The others were already chanting, everyone but Chris, who was very still. Didn't say anything that I remember. I ate my first button and then the rest was history."

"What do you mean, history?" Fernando asked.

"I mean the meeting went by the book, the same routine it always followed," Boros said. "I started my usual trip—the visions and the colors. It was kind of a bummer trip, because I kept seeing my wife's face in different colors telling me she wanted a divorce, over and over. Then, sometime later, I heard loud voices that brought me out of my vision. I saw Antonio, the big guy, wrestling with Doctor Ziggy over by Chris. Looked like Antonio had a hold of Chris and was doing something that Ziggy was trying to stop. Then everyone started to yell and I lost track. I got a sick stomach from the peyote and started puking behind the fire circle. I don't remember, but I must have driven home that night, because I remember waking up on my sofa at home the next morning when Doctor Ziggy called to tell me what happened."

"So Ziggy told you what happened after the fact," Fernando said. "That's the version of events you got—Ziggy's version."

"Yes, I suppose so, it was his version," Boros said. "Because back at the fire circle I had no idea what was happening."

"Because you were incapacitated...." Fernando added.

"Yes, I had no idea until he called," Boros agreed.

"And he told you that Antonio had choked or strangled Chris?"

Boros nodded again.

"Have you talked to either of the other two people who were at the fire circle that night, Mary Logan or Tom Lujan?" Fernando asked. "If so, did they corroborate Ziggy's version of events?"

"No, so far I've only talked to the detective and now you," Boros said. "I don't really know the other two. We've never talked much."

"So you're repeating Ziggy's version," Fernando said, mostly to himself.

# 6

On his way home Fernando remembered the last time he'd seen Tom Lujan. It was one evening last Spring at the La Choza restaurant, where he and Estelle had gone for dinner. They bumped into Lujan as they were leaving, he recalled. They chatted for a few minutes near the doorway. Lujan wasn't in the best of health, suffering from heart and breathing problems. Lujan told them he was living in a friend's guest house in La Cienega. They talked about staying in touch. Lujan jotted down his cell phone number on a slip of paper and handed it to Fernando. What happened to that slip of paper? That was the question.

Still wondering, Fernando pulled into his driveway on Acequia Madre and parked next to their garage. As soon as he walked into their house he headed for his study. He looked through all the drawers in his desk, riffling through piles of old bills, newspaper clippings and other crap he'd saved for one reason or another. No luck. Then he remembered his old address book, which he hadn't used in months. Maybe he'd stuck Lujan's slip of paper in there.

Since the address book wasn't in his desk, he went over to his closet and flipped through the stacks of folders and photo albums. He found the dog-eared address book under a box of old Polaroid photos of his two daughters, Flavia and Adela, when they were young. With its leather cover cracked and coming unglued, its pages torn and yellowed, it was no wonder he'd tossed the damn thing in the closet for storage. Good thing he'd kept it, because the Lujan paper was tucked neatly inside the back cover. Bingo.

Fernando sat down at his desk and dialed Lujan's number.

After several rings someone clicked on but instead of a voice Fernando heard crashing noises, as if the phone had been dropped on the floor.

"Hello..." came a faint, raspy voice Fernando didn't recognize.

"Tom? Tom Lujan?"

"Yeah..." the voice wheezed.

"This is Fernando Lopez calling," Fernando said.

"Who...?"

"Fernando Lopez, we were in the same class at Santa Fe High," Fernando said. "I used to be a Santa Fe Police detective."

Silence. "Yeah, what do you want?"

"I'd like to ask you a few questions about what you saw in the fire circle at Rancho Nirvana a couple of days ago," Fernando said. "The day Chris Chabot died."

More silence.

"Do you remember what happened?"

"Don't remember. Didn't see anything," the raspy voice came through the phone.

"Is that what Doctor Ziggy told you to say?" Fernando asked.

"Listen...I don't know what you're after, but I got nothing for you," Lujan gasped. "I'm a sick man. I need a new liver, plus my lungs are shot. Now leave me alone."

"Wait—did you see Antonio Blake kill Chris Chabot?" Fernando blurted out, trying to get an answer to at least one question. Too late. Lujan clicked off and didn't answer when Fernando hit the redial button.

Pissed, Fernando opened his laptop and searched for Lujan's address in La Cienega. He found it quickly and then got up to go pay a visit to the rasping, reluctant man. Then he thought twice about his decision. Maybe he got all he needed from Lujan. At least for the moment. He could always pay Lujan a visit later, if he needed to. First, though, he wanted to check out Mary Logan and see what she could add to help clarify what had transpired in the fire circle that night at Rancho Nirvana.

Before leaving, he grabbed his Smith & Wesson on the top shelf of the closet in his study. Whoever answered the phone at Mary Logan's house when he called earlier sounded downright unfriendly, so he wanted to be prepared. Then he headed for the kitchen. While locking the kitchen door, his cell phone rang. He stopped immediately when he saw who was calling.

"Antonio...where the hell are you?"

"I'm in Taos, staying at the Sagebrush Inn," Antonio said, matter-of-factly. He seemed much too calm, given the situation.

Fernando sat down at the kitchen table, shaking his head. "You're in a lot of trouble down here, Antonio. They think you killed Chris Chabot."

Antonio didn't respond.

"Did you kill Chabot?" Fernando asked.

"I don't know, I'm trying to sort things out," Antonio said. "I could use your help."

"What can I do?" Fernando asked and immediately regretted it.

"Can you come up to Taos?" Antonio responded.

Fernando sighed. The last thing he wanted to do was drive up to Taos, but this was Antonio. What could he do? "Okay...what room are you in?"

"Four nineteen, in the older part of the inn," Antonio said. "On the south side of the original courtyard. You know, the haunted side."

Fernando did know, although he didn't want to revisit that memory. "I'm on my way. Should be thee in a couple of hours."

After Antonio clicked off, Fernando gathered his wits and made a mental list of things he needed to do before leaving. First he wrote a note to Estelle saying he had to make a quick trip to Taos, because Antonio was hiding out at the Sagebrush and asked for help and that he may have to spend the night in Taos, depending on Antonio's situation. Then he packed the small overnight bag and shaving kit he usually took in these situations and carried them out to the Cherokee. He tossed the bags in the rear compartment and locked his Smith & Wesson in the glove compartment, just in case he needed it.

Ready, he locked the kitchen door and climbed into his Cherokee. He drove down to the Paseo and around to the entrance to Highway 285/84. Not wasting any time, he sped past the Tesuque exits and the Santa Fe Opera, slowing down as he came into the Pojoaque commercial strip. He thought momentarily about taking the colorful high road to Taos, through the ancient villages of Chimayo, Truchas, and Las Trampas. Problem was, that would take an extra half hour, at least. He didn't want to waste any time. He wanted to hear Antonio's side of the story before someone recognized Antonio from the APB Manny had sent out.

So he opted for the low road to Taos, which followed alongside the Rio Grande from Española to Taos. Once through the clutter of Española he began to relax as he followed the river, with green triangular hills on either side of the river. Nearing Pilar he began to see rafters and kayakers on the river. The rafts and kayaks came bouncing down through the rapids off to his left, sometimes crashing in a wall of foam. Then he entered the long curve that climbed up to Ranchos de Taos and the famous San Francisco de Asis Catholic Church that had been photographed and painted by a zillion artists, including Georgia O'Keeffe.

Entering Taos he saw the 14,000-foot peaks of the Taos Mountains straight ahead, a spectacular view that always cheered him. He came quickly to the historic Sagebrush Inn on his left, a hundred-year-old sprawling adobe building with multiple wings and courtyards. He'd stayed at the Sagebrush many times, on many cases, most recently on his Taos vendetta case. Great bar, good food, and tolerable rooms, if you weren't too fussy and didn't look too closely. Which he didn't.

Fernando turned left into the main entrance to the Sagebrush. He bypassed the registration building and parked next to the oldest part of the three-sided building, built around a central courtyard. He noticed Antonio's Wrangler was nowhere to be seen in any of the parking areas. Had Antonio hidden the Jeep on the grounds somewhere...or gone to do an errand, or possibly moved to a more private motel, somewhere off the beaten path? Possibly, but he would need to check Antonio's room first before deciding what to do.

He climbed out of his Cherokee and walked across the gravel and dried grass of the courtyard, under three tall cottonwood trees with wild and jagged branches that cast ominous shadows in front of him. Reminded him of three gigantic witches blotting out the sun and blocking access to the southern and western wings of the Sagebrush. From the edge of the courtyard he spotted Antonio's room, 419, toward the middle of the southern wing.

Fernando recognized the rickety old wooden staircases that led to the rooms on the second floor from his previous experience on the Painted Skull Ranch case. The stairs and walkway, painted a chocolate brown, contrasted with the tan stucco of the building. The stairs creaked as he began to climb, sounding like the whole damn wooden scaffolding was about to collapse with him on it. Still, he kept climbing until he reached the second floor, where he stopped and leaned against the side of the building, hoping the creaking would stop. It did. Then he moved on down the walkway to room 419 and knocked lightly on the door, not wanting to call attention to his presence if anyone happened to be in the courtyard below.

The door opened quickly, revealing a bedraggled Antonio. Wearing jeans and a gray sweatshirt, with tired eyes and wild hair, the big man almost blocked the entire doorway. He stood six feet, eight inches tall and weighed two hundred and eighty pounds. He did not look like a happy man.

Antonio yanked Fernando inside. Then he poked his head outside the door and looked left and right. He motioned to his left. "Don't worry, the haunted room is a couple doors down."

Fernando laughed. "I forgot about the haunted room. I had enough of that the last time I was here."

Antonio grunted and sat down on a desk chair in the corner of the room, across from the two double beds. Even sitting, Antonio was huge.

"Tell me, why did you start going to Rancho Nirvana?" Fernando asked. "You know Ziggy is a phony. He's a drug addict and a dope dealer. He's no more a doctor than you or I."

"Yeah, but he has access to peyote, which I needed at the time," Antonio replied. "Peyote really helps with my Post Traumatic Stress Disorder. One of the few things that does."

Fernando nodded. "I heard from Manny that you were having problems again with the PTSD. I'm sorry to hear that. You look exhausted. Have you been getting any sleep since this happened?"

"Not much," Antonio said. "Usually I have bad nightmares when I try to sleep. Sometimes even during the day I get these daymares, or whatever they're called. Bad flashbacks of my time in Iraq."

"And taking peyote in the fire circle was helping you?" Fernando asked.

"Yeah, like I said, peyote is one of the few things that help. Sometimes after a ceremony I could go several days without a nightmare, but they always returned sooner or later. So I would do it again. And again."

Fernando decided to not beat around the bush any longer. "So what happened that night in the fire circle. You said you didn't know if you killed Chris Chabot. What does that mean?"

Antonio shook his head. "Just that. I can't remember. The ceremony started at sundown. There were four of us at first, in addition to Doctor Ziggy. Ziggy passed around the bag of peyote. Each of us took a button and ate it. Right away I got sick to my stomach, and then my visions began."

"Like a nightmare?" Fernando asked.

Antonio nodded. "I saw myself back in Iraq with flashes of red and then lots of white smoke. My Jeep crashed and then I was trying to get out of the Jeep and run away. At some point during my visions I remember seeing Chris join the circle, helped by Doctor Ziggy's assistant, Joey. I didn't pay much attention to Chris because I was getting more and more paranoid. I was afraid of being left behind in the smoke. When a shooter behind a wall started shooting at us, I jumped up and charged. I started to shout just as I reached out to grab the shooter. Suddenly my vision flashed and I found myself holding Chris by the neck, not the shooter, and shaking him. I think I was trying to get him to wake up and help me out of my vision—away from the smoke and the shooter. Next thing I knew it was the ten o'clock water call and Doctor Ziggy was yelling at me, accusing me of something–"

"Wait--you say Chris was asleep, or appeared to be asleep?" Fernando interrupted Antonio's narrative.

Antonio nodded. He got up from the chair and walked over to the door and peeked out the eyehole. Then he walked back to the chair and sat back down and continued. "When I realized what had happened, and that Chris was dead, I took off. I managed to run down to my Jeep and drive back to Santa Fe. I stopped at Ihop for something to eat and lots of coffee, and then I drove up to Taos in the dark. I stopped at the Rio Grande Gorge Visitor Center and slept in the Jeep for a couple of hours and then drove to the Sagebrush. Remember, people always used to say the Sagebrush was the best place to have an affair or hide out? I guess that's why I stopped here. I needed a place to hide out."

Fernando brooded on Antonio's story for a couple of minutes before speaking. Then he said, "Question is—was Chris already dead when you grabbed him? From what you just said, it sounds like he might have been."

Antonio did not respond.

"On the other hand, Manny seems to believe Ziggy and the others— that you killed Chris," Fernando said. "That's why he considers you the primary suspect."

Again Antonio did not respond.

"And who's this Joey guy, Ziggy's assistant," Fernando asked.

Antonio frowned. "Joey Alhambra. He supplies the drugs, among other things. Peyote and fentanyl and whatever else Ziggy wants."

Fernando nodded.

"What do you think I should do?" Antonio asked.

"Well, you could come back to Santa Fe and try to clear your name, or you could stay up here somewhere and give me time to find out who killed Chris," Fernando replied.

Antonio thought about that for a moment. "If I come back, they'll probably arrest me."

"Probably."

"Then I'll stay here, but you better find the killer fast before I lose patience," Antonio said.

Fernando checked his watch. "Will do, but right now I'm starving. I never had lunch today."

# 7

Fernando followed Antonio down the rickety wooden stairway. The steps creaked and groaned as the big man stomped down into the courtyard. By the sound Fernando once again thought the whole damn structure was about to collapse. He jumped down from the last step, eager to be off the stairway before it imploded. He breathed a bit easier when he reached the ground, noticing Antonio halfway across the courtyard, seemingly unconcerned about the flimsy stairway.

They walked through the patio and entered the Sagebrush Grill through its patio door. The Grill looked exactly like he remembered it: plank floor with heavy wooden beams holding up the vigas on the ceiling. Classic Taos. They sat at one of the tables in the far corner on heavy wooden chairs, clunky and uncomfortable. Fernando ordered one of the Sagebrush Grill's famous breakfast burritos with red chile, while Antonio ordered what he always ordered, the combination plate with one of nearly everything on the menu. The big man ate like a horse.

After they finished the server, a middle-aged woman with gray hair and glasses wearing a colorful red apron, brought them the check. She handed the check to Antonio, who handed it to Fernando, who laughed. "My pleasure," he said, knowing from experience that Antonio never paid.

Just then they heard the nightly music start up next door in the Cantina. "Let's get some beers and listen to the music," Antonio said.

Fernando checked his watch. It was too late to drive back to Santa Fe in the dark, so why not? What the hell? "Okay, I'll get a room for the night."

"No, you can take the other bed in my room, why spend money if you don't have to?" Antonio asked. The big man was notoriously cheap. He never spent money on anything unless he absolutely had to.

With that, they walked into the Cantina, a long rectangular room with a beautiful hand-carved bar running along one wall. Otherwise the room looked identical to the Grill, just smaller, with a plank floor and heavy wooden posts holding up the viga ceiling. A group of three musicians stood at the front of the room, near the entrance, playing some old county favorites, Bob Wills and Hank Williams, intermixed with some of their original tunes. Antonio found a semi-dark corner table in the back of the room, where they could be unseen, anonymous. They hoped.

A young woman with red hair, a nose ring, and tattoos on both arms came up to them as soon as they sat down. "What can I get you fellers?"

"I'll have a Modelo draft," Fernando said.

"Make that two," Antonio added.

While the country trio wailed away up front, Fernando and Antonio sipped their beers. "We'll need to stay in touch," Fernando said. "So why don't you call me every day at high Noon. I'll make sure I'm free every day at Noon to take your call. You can turn your phone off right after we talk, okay?"

Antonio nodded, listening to the music. It was clear he didn't want to talk about his legal situation.

Later, after a couple more beers, Fernando paid the check and the two of them walked back through the Grill to the patio, deserted now except for a lone worker cleaning tables and moving dirty dishes inside. They entered the dark patio, ringed with strings of feeble lights strung from the trees that did a poor job of holding back the massive darkness around and above them. When they approached the rickety stairway, Fernando stood back and waited until Antonio reached the top and stepped onto the walkway.

Antonio looked down at Fernando. "Aren't you coming?"

"Just waiting for you to reach the top," Fernando said. "That stairway looks like an accident waiting to happen." Antonio was young enough to believe he was invulnerable—Fernando was old enough to know that whatever bad could happen, would happen.

Holding on to the railing, Fernando tip-toed up the stairway and followed Antonio to his room. The big man went into the bathroom to get ready for bed, while Fernando sat on the nearest bed and texted Estelle, which he'd neglected to do earlier. Not good, because Estelle expected him to keep her informed about his whereabouts in a timely fashion, an agreement they'd made back when he was a Santa Fe Police detective. He preferred to text rather than call, so that he wouldn't have to listen to Estelle reprimand him for not retiring once and for all.

He typed: "Spending the night at the Sagebrush with Antonio. Back tomorrow morning." He would make amends tomorrow when he returned.

After that, he set his phone on the nightstand and took off his boots. Suddenly he felt exhausted, nothing left in the tank. He collapsed on top of the bed without bothering to take off his clothes. Moments later he heard Antonio come out of the bathroom and turn off the lights and then climb into the other bed. He heard a lone coyote howling mournfully out on the mesa as he drifted off to the land of dreams.

Again Fernando found himself in the darkened house trying to find his way out. Somewhere in the darkness the woman cried softly, stopping for a few seconds and then starting again. He fumbled along a wall trying to find a light switch but found nothing. Thunder rumbled outside, followed by the boom of a lightning strike that shook the house and illuminated a window at the end of a shadowy hallway. Maybe the hallway led to a door, a way out. He leaped forward toward the window but stumbled on an area rug and pitched forward onto the floor. The rug stank of mold and water damage. He crawled forward on all fours so as not to fall again. He smelled something else now, an acrid smell that pierced his nostrils. Fire?

"Ahhhhhhhhhhh!" someone was shouting...in the house?

No, it was Antonio in the next bed, Fernando realized as he awoke, rising to the level of consciousness. Something was wrong with Antonio, who continued screaming and thrashing in the bed.

Fernando sat up in bed. He tried to clear his head. Was Antonio injured? Then it occurred to him. Of course. The big man was suffering from his Post Traumatic Stress Disorder.

"Hey—you okay?" Fernando asked, climbing out of bed and moving over to Antonio's bed.

Suddenly Antonio's legs kicked so violently they flung off the blankets. He appeared to be trying to run. "Get out...run!" he shouted.

Fernando grabbed Antonio by the shoulders. "Wake up, you're just having a nightmare."

In response Antonio flung his right arm hard, hitting Fernando in the chest and knocking him clean off the bed. He landed flat on his ass, the jolt shooting a wave of pain up his spine. "Oww, goddamnit!" Fernando barked.

On the bed Antonio started to mumble. He seemed to be waking up slowly. Eventually he sat up in bed and grabbed his head with both hands. He turned his head from side to side and then pushed back the shock of black hair that kept falling over his eyes. He looked over the side of the bed spying Fernando sitting on the carpet. "Where am I? What are you doing here? What's going on?"

"You were having a nightmare," Fernando responded. "You're

staying at the Sagebrush Inn in Taos, remember. I just spent the night because I didn't want to drive home in the dark."

Antonio threw his legs over the side of the bed and stared at Fernando. "But what are you doing down there?"

Fernando laughed. "You slugged me. This is where I landed."

Antonio rubbed the back of his neck with his left hand. "Jesus, I don't remember anything."

"Don't worry about it," Fernando said. "I had a nightmare too. Maybe it's this place. Or the haunted room next door."

Antonio shook his head. "No, it's my PTSD. Lately it's been a flashback of the time our convoy ran over an IED on the road into Fallujah. We had to run for cover, dragging or carrying those who couldn't walk. We were out in the open, exposed. Incoming from every direction, a fucking nightmare. I don't know how any of us made it out alive."

"IED?" Fernando asked.

"Improvised explosive device." Antonio explained. "They would bury them in the roads. The fucking things were everywhere."

Moving slowly and carefully, Fernando picked himself up and sat on his bed facing Antonio. "There must be men's groups in Santa Fe that could help you—groups that focus on Post Traumatic Stress Disorder."

"Yeah, I've been there, done that," Antonio said, waving his hand. "I've been in two groups over the years, even saw a shrink once. Fact is, nothing works as well as the drugs. By drugs I mean mescaline and peyote, the hallucinogens. It's a way you can enter a space where there's no stress or anxiety. I can't really explain it better than that. It sets you free to experience the here and now."

"Why don't you become a member of the Native American Church," Fernando asked.

"I am a member," Antonio said, "but the nearest group is down in Galisteo and the leader, its Road Chief, is unreliable. He disappears for months at a time. Not as if I can find a meeting whenever I need one."

"Can't you take it by yourself?" Fernando asked. "Do you have a supply of peyote?"

Antonio nodded. "Sure, I have a supply of peyote, but it's not the same. You need a group...just in case."

Just in case of what, Fernando wanted to know but didn't ask. Instead, he went into the bathroom and washed his face, trying to wake up. He made himself a cup of coffee in the coffeemaker on the bureau and put on his boots. One of the benefits of sleeping in all your clothes is that you wake up ready for action.

"There's two cups here, you want me to make you a cup of coffee?"

Fernando asked Antonio, who was getting dressed in the bathroom.

"No, I'm going for a run first," Antonio said, pulling a pair of running shoes out of the closet.

"Okay, then I'll see you later when things calm down," Fernando said. "I'm going over to the Grill for breakfast on my way back to Santa Fe. Remember to call me every day at Noon and I'll give you a report, whatever I've found out about Chabot and who might have killed him."

Antonio saluted as Fernando walked out of the room and closed the door behind him.

## 8

On the way back to Santa Fe Fernando decided to take his sweet time. Since he had no reason to hurry, he might as well relax and enjoy the countryside. So instead of the faster low road to Taos, he took the high road through the Sangre de Cristo Mountains. He drove his Cherokee out of the Sagebrush Inn parking lot and took an immediate left onto Highway 518, which took him into Ranchos de Taos and past the Jesus Nazareno Cemetery. Just a few months earlier he and Antonio had brought Jack Lacy—the so-called Santa Fe Assassin—to Jesus Nazareno so he could visit the grave of his old friend Dennis Hopper.

Once past Jesus Nazareno and the memories of Jack Lacy, who he would like to forget, Fernando headed south into the mountains. The mountain road jutted over to Highway 75 and then Highway 76, taking him through a series of old picturesque Hispanic villages that looked like they hadn't changed in decades. First Peñasco, followed by Trampas, Truchas, Cordova, and Chimayo, all picture perfect in the bright New Mexico sunshine. He loved the villages; he'd often wondered what his life would have been like had he lived in one of the villages.

When he came to the junction of Highway 285/84, Fernando hit the gas. He roared through the Pojoaque strip and up the Tesuque hill into Santa Fe. He drove directly home, not stopping for gas or anything else. He checked the clock on the dash as he pulled into his driveway on Acequia Madre. Quarter past eleven. It had taken him nearly two hours to drive back to Santa Fe on the high road to Taos. No wonder he always took the low road.

Fernando parked in front of the garage and climbed out of his Cherokee. He walked across the patio to the kitchen door and opened the door. With Estelle working, he had the run of the house. First thing, he took a hot shower and changed clothes. Then he came back to the kitchen and heated up a plate of leftovers for lunch. Looked like enchiladas left over from a recent meal, at least he hoped it was recent anyway. After making himself a cup of coffee in his Keurig, he took everything outside to his bench on their patio.

Fernando leaned back against the side of the house and closed his eyes. It had been an exhausting twenty-four hours and he had nothing to show for it, nada. Relaxed, he drifted off to a state that wasn't exactly sleep but wasn't exactly wakefulness either. The relaxation took him to a semi-conscious realm of daydreams and imagination. He watched a dream video of Antonio picking up Chris Chabot by the neck and shaking him so hard his head snapped off and fell to the ground while the headless body dropped heavily on the sandy bottom of Apache Canyon. The image of Chabot's head rolling on the ground jolted him back to consciousness.

Fernando stretched his arms and back muscles and tried to relax. When he reached for his plate of food, he noticed flies were swarming on and around the plate. He pushed the food aside and just drank his coffee. He would grab a snack later, something to hold him to dinnertime.

Sitting there, more or less awake, it occurred to him that he should call Manny to see if there were any new developments in the Chabot murder case. So he went inside and disposed the food, putting the dishes in the sink. Then he sat down at the kitchen table and called Manny, who answered right away on his cell phone. "What's up, Fernando?"

"Hey, Manny, I'm just calling to see if there's anything new in the Chabot case," Fernando said.

Manny sighed. "No, we're still waiting for the Medical Examiner's report. As far as I know, no one's reported seeing Antonio. Have you found him?"

Fernando didn't answer at first.

"Would you tell me if you had seen him?" Manny asked.

"Me? No, I have no idea where he is," Fernando lied through his teeth. "Why would I?"

"Well, because he's your best friend, that's why," Manny replied.

Fernando let that slide. He considered. Finally he said, "Just remember, he's your friend too. He's saved both of our asses more times than I can remember, back when Antonio and I were on the force."

"I know, but I have to do my fucking job," Manny said.

"Is Antonio still your prime suspect?" Fernando asked.

"I got nothing else," Manny said and clicked off.

Fernando held his cell phone for a few seconds before putting it down, surprised that Manny had ended the call so abruptly. Manny was getting defensive, a little pissy even.

Since most of the afternoon remained, he decided to pay Mary Logan a visit. Whoever answered her phone yesterday wasn't particularly friendly, so why not show up at her door? Maybe she would be alone. It was worth a try.

Fernando glanced at his notebook to check Mary Logan's address on Antonio Lane, just before the village of Agua Fria. Before leaving, he debated whether to take his Smith & Wesson. He decided against it because he didn't want to provoke anyone, especially the hothead who'd answered the phone when he'd called earlier. Better to play it cool, be friendly, try to get Logan to talk about what she saw the night Chris Chabot was murdered.

So he locked the house and climbed into his Cherokee. Taking the fastest route, he drove down Acequia Madre, turned left on the Paseo and took it directly to Saint Francis Drive. Then he turned right and shot down to Agua Fria Street. It was slow going on Agua Fria, lots of cars and stoplights. He almost missed Antonio Lane, a nondescript little street with a few houses scattered along both sides of the street. He found Logan's house halfway down the street, an L-shaped adobe with a flat roof squatting in a big dirt yard devoid of grass or flowers. Nothing but a few patches of weeds in the dusty yard.

Fernando turned into the drive and pulled up behind a beat-up Ford Fiesta and an old rusted Dodge Ram pickup that looked like it had been abandoned years ago. Taking his time, he surveyed the scene. The house, like the yard, had seen better days. The stucco on the adobe had cracked and crumbled in multiple places, revealing the bare adobe underneath. One side window was broken and had been replaced with a plastic sheet. And the blue paint on most of the doors and windowsills had faded badly to a dusty gray color, made worse by flaking and peeling from too many years in the hot New Mexico sun.

Wary, Fernando climbed out of his Cherokee and walked slowly to the front door. For a moment he regretted not bringing his Smith & Wesson. He opened a flimsy screen door and knocked gently on the metal door. When no one responded, he knocked harder and harder, finally banging on the door. Finally the door flew open and an angry young man appeared on the other side, a skinny redhead with a bad complexion and an even worse attitude.

"What the fuck?" the kid shouted. "Why are you banging on my door? What do you want?"

Fernando stood back from the door, unnerved by the kid's hostility. "I'm here to see Mary Logan. Is she home?"

The kid kicked the screen door open and stepped outside screaming,

"No! You can't see her. She doesn't need any more of the shit you're selling. It's killing her. Get out of here or I'll kill you!"

"Wait, you're mistaking me for someone else," Fernando tried to explain, realizing the kid was mistaking him for someone else, probably Joey Alhambra, Ziggy's drug dealer. "I'm just here to talk—" Fernando started to say, but the kid darted forward and shoved him hard with both hands. Fernando lost his balance and fell backwards, landing on his ass in the dust. Ironically, right next to the welcome mat.

"Get out!" the kid screamed. "Tell Joey to stay away. Tell him to stop bringing that shit over here."

Fernando struggled to get to his feet. He managed to roll over on his hands and knees and then managed to stand. When he did, the kid threw a haymaker that clipped him on the side of his face and sent him sprawling backward. Again he landed on his ass. This time harder.

"You understand now?" the kid asked, launching a kick aimed for Fernando's abdomen.

Fernando grabbed the kid's leg and pulled as hard as he could.

The kid screamed as his other leg went out from under him. He landed on the slab porch cursing, but sprang up quickly and lunged at Fernando. The kid was wiry and mad as hell.

No problem. At 180 pounds of solid muscle, Fernando outweighed the skinny little punk by a good forty or fifty pounds. He waited until the kid was within reach and then grabbed him by the neck and pressed his thumbs into the kid's neck. When the kid began to choke, Fernando shoved hard and sent the kid sprawling to his right, off the porch. Instantly Fernando jumped on the kid and pinned both his arms to the ground so he couldn't throw any more punches.

"Let me go, you fucker!" the kid spit out.

Fernando had had enough. He slapped the kid across the face so hard that the whole side of his face turned red. Dazed, the kid started gurgling out a string of words that were incomprehensible.

"Listen, you little prick, I have nothing to do with Joey," Fernando hissed. "I'm here to talk to Mary Logan, whether you like it or not. If you don't stop this, I'm going to give you a beating that you won't forget. Just try to hit me again. It would be a pleasure to beat the hell out of you."

Fernando felt the kid relax underneath him. The kid turned his head and looked away.

Fernando stood, brushing the dust off his clothing. The kid, out of breath, motioned toward the house.

Fernando took that as an invitation, so he opened the door and walked into the house. Dark, with all its curtains drawn, the house reminded him of the nightmare he kept having. What did that mean? Was it some kind of omen? Fernando wasn't superstitious, but then again he wasn't not superstitious. He just didn't know and was not afraid to admit it.

"Miss Logan?" he called out, standing in the middle of a small front room with a plaid sofa and a couple of chairs facing a portable television hooked to an old-fashioned rabbit ears antennae.

Somewhere in the house he heard a noise, a rocking noise. Then a woman's voice, barely audible: "Who's there? I need my medication. Please."

Fernando walked down a short hallway into a dimly lit kitchen, its one window shrouded by a heavy plastic curtain. He found an ancient, emaciated woman sitting at a rickety wooden kitchen table. Tiny, with tangled gray hair and a deeply lined face, she looked like she weighed no more than eighty pounds. At the moment she was rubbing her hands together on the kitchen table and rocking back and forth in her wooden table chair, which creaked as she rocked. Back and forth, obsessively. Looked like the woman had some mental issues.

"Are you okay?" Fernando asked.

"I need my meds...please," the woman said, her voice no more than a whisper. "Did Joey send you with my meds?" she asked hopefully, holding out her tiny wrinkled hand.

Fernando shook his head. "No, I'm here to ask what you saw at Rancho Nirvana the night Chris Chabot was murdered. Are you Mary Logan?"

"Mary, that's me," she said, starting to rock again.

"Did you see who strangled Chris Chabot?" Fernando tried again.

"No, I was too scared," she said.

"Too scared?"

"They were fighting," she said.

"Who was fighting?"

"Chris was arguing with Joey and Doctor Ziggy," she said. "My son dropped me off early, before the ceremony, so I could get my meds from Joey. When I walked in Chris and Doctor Ziggy were arguing and yelling at each other. Joey too. I was scared. I wanted my medication, but I had to wait until they were done arguing before I got them from Joey."

Trying to follow her story, Fernando asked, "What happened when the ceremony began?"

She shook her head. "I don't remember. It was like a dream. I took my meds and then ate the peyote button when they passed around the bag. Lotta people talking and later on yelling at each other. Me, I saw the spirit of my departed husband and told him I forgave him for all the bad things he done to me and hope he forgave me for the one thing I did to him. I think that cheered him up a bit because he'd been in the dark place lately. He knows what I done to him, me and the boy, Sammy."

Fernando could not care less about what she and her son had done to the father, so he changed the subject. "What about Chris? Do you remember seeing him in the fire circle during the ceremony?"

She thought for a moment and then said, "No, because he was real quiet. He didn't say anything during the ceremony. I guess that's why I don't remember him."

"Was he dead?" Fernando asked bluntly.

"Departed? Why would he be in the fire circle if he was departed?" she asked. "That's a dumb question, you know. Plus I need my medication. Did Joey give it to you?"

Fernando had enough. "Listen," he said, as kindly as possible. "You need to listen to your son. Go to rehab...let trained professionals help you break the habit before it kills you."

Mary did not respond.

"Here, call me if you can remember anything else about that night," Fernando said, handing her one of his cards.

With that Fernando left the room and walked outside into the fresh air, which never felt so good. The son was nowhere to be found. Hiding somewhere, or maybe watching from one of the rear windows in the house.

Eager to get away, Fernando climbed into his Cherokee and headed home.

# 9

When Fernando awoke, he found Estelle's side of the bed empty. He could hear her working in the kitchen, preparing breakfast. He sat up in bed for a moment to clear his head and then pulled on his jeans and shuffled barefoot down the hallway to the kitchen. Estelle had finished breakfast and was in the process of packing lunch for her work at the Saint Francis Immigrant Outreach Program. She stopped what she was doing and turned to Fernando, doing a double-take. She shook her head sadly when she saw his swollen face.

"Oh, Fernando, what have you done now?" Estelle asked, shaking her head in disgust. "You're eye's all black and blue. Don't you know, you're too old to get into fist fights or however you got that. You're supposed to be retired."

"I am retired, really. I'm just helping out Antonio," Fernando said, feeling his left cheek. It was a bit sore, he had to admit.

Estelle sighed. "I know you won't listen to me. You'll do what you will do, as always. Just remember, you're not young anymore. You need to take better care of yourself."

They went round and round for a few minutes until Estelle tired of arguing and announced she was leaving for work. After she left, Fernando went back to the master bath and looked in the mirror, something he rarely if ever did. Sure enough, the left side of his face was slightly swollen, with a bruise that wasn't exactly a black eye but close enough to cause consternation. He cursed to himself. He should have been more careful. He should have knocked Sammy senseless before the kid had a chance to strike the first blow.

Fernando finished dressing and then went back to the kitchen. Too groggy to eat, he poured himself a cup of coffee and took it out to the patio to think. He took out his notebook and re-read the few notes he'd taken. The three witnesses he'd talked to, even though high on peyote at the time and probably not credible on a witness stand, seemed to agree on several things. First, that Chris Chabot seemed out of it at the beginning of the peyote ceremony. George Boros described Chabot as "very still" and added that he "didn't say anything." Mary Logan described Chabot as "real quiet" and agreed that he didn't speak during the ceremony. These descriptions matched what Antonio had said, that Chabot "appeared to be asleep." Only Tom Lujan refused to comment, apparently on orders from Doctor Ziggy himself.

So the first question became: was Chabot already dead when the peyote ceremony began? If so, then Antonio was likely off the hook, especially since Chabot had argued with Ziggy and Alhambra before the ceremony started.

The second question concerned the role of Alhambra, Ziggy's assistant. Mary Logan said she'd seen Chabot arguing with Ziggy and Alhambra before the ceremony began. And Antonio said Alhambra actually helped or possibly carried Chabot to his seat at the beginning of the ceremony.

To get answers Fernando would have to return to Rancho Nirvana and again question Ziggy, which he didn't look forward to. The fast-talking con man rubbed him the wrong way.

After finishing his coffee he went back inside the kitchen and searched the refrigerator for leftovers he could eat for breakfast. He found nothing that looked particularly appetizing, so he made himself a plate of scrambled eggs and toast, washed down by another cup of coffee. After he cleaned up the kitchen he took a third cup of coffee into his study and read the day's *Independent*. The one story about the death of Chris Chabot, buried on page four, reported only that police were still searching for a person of interest in the suspected homicide. Doctor Ziggy was mentioned as a 'naturopathic therapist.' That made Fernando laugh. What the hell was a naturopathic therapist anyway?

Fernando lounged around the house brooding until his cell phone rang.

When he checked his watch, he saw that it was already Noon. Antonio was right on time. The big man had agreed to call every day at Noon to keep him informed.

"Thanks for calling, Antonio," he answered.

"I'm coming back," Antonio said. "I'm gonna deal with Ziggy and Alhambra my own way."

"Wait. What? I don't think it's such a good idea for you to come back right now," Fernando said, taken aback by Antonio's announcement.

"I think I'm getting close to finding out who killed Chabot. So far it looks like he may already have been dead when the ceremony started."

"Good," Antonio said. "Then I'll help you finish. I'm tired of staying at the fucking Sagebrush. Place depresses me."

"Are you sure about this?" Fernando asked. "I mean, you're still the number one person of interest."

"I'm sure. I meditated for a long time last night. I relived the experience...and now I'm sure I didn't kill Chris."

"I don't think you killed him either, but you should at least call Raoul Garcia just in case they charge you," Fernando said.

"Yeah, I did. I called him yesterday. I'll see you soon," Antonio said and clicked off before Fernando could respond.

Now Fernando was worried. Not so much that Antonio would be apprehended, because Antonio knew how to keep a low profile. No, he was worried about what the big man would do to Ziggy. For years Antonio Blake had been the 'enforcer' of the Santa Fe Police Department. At six feet, eight inches and two hundred and eighty pounds, Antonio was extraordinarily strong. When angered, Antonio could be brutal. He could literally tear Ziggy apart, limb by limb. Which would get him in even more trouble with Manny.

Feeling a sense of urgency, Fernando decided to leave right away for Rancho Nirvana. For a moment he debated whether to take his Smith & Wesson, but again decided against it. Why precipitate more gun violence? He'd had his fill after thirty years of police work and another five as a private investigator. Now he called himself a fixer and tried to avoid involving guns. Whenever possible.

So he locked up the house and once again headed out Old Santa Fe Trail to the Old Las Vegas Highway. The last signs of the city faded away as he passed the turnoff to El Dorado, one of Santa Fe's growing bedroom communities. When he came to Bobcat Bite, one of his favorite burger restaurants in years past, Fernando realized he'd forgotten to eat lunch. He decided to stop there on the way back to Santa Fe, after he'd confronted Ziggy.

Minutes later he turned right into Apache Canyon and followed the road around to Rancho Nirvana. He parked next to a black Cadillac Escalade with dark windows, always a sign of trouble, and a beat-up L.L. Bean Subaru Outback from an earlier decade. Looking around, he didn't see a soul on the expansive grounds, so he quickly climbed the flagstone path to the main house with its long veranda and pitched roof. He stepped up on the veranda, furnished with several bamboo rocking chairs and a wooden bench. He didn't bother to knock. Instead, he opened a rickety screen door and stepped inside the large front room with its rows of church pews facing a podium and white board. From there he heard muffled voices coming from a small room off to the right that looked like an office.

"Hello," Fernando said, walking into the office.

Ziggy sat in a reclining chair at an old mahogany desk talking on his cell phone. He nodded to Fernando.

In the rear of the room sat a slick, thuggish looking man who appeared out of place in rustic Rancho Nirvana. Wearing stretch golf pants and a Polo shirt, the man had short but immaculately coiffed black hair. Even more off-putting was his face–it looked smashed in, like he'd taken too many punches in a career as a boxer. His nose, lips, and chin were flattened. Joey Alhambra?

Ziggy finished his conversation and hung up the phone. "Well, now, if it isn't Detective Fernando Lopez again. Once a cop, always a cop, you can tell by the smell. Man, I hadn't seen you in twenty years, and suddenly you start showing up at my door every time I turn around. Last time you were here I answered all your questions, told you what I know about what happened to Chris and sent you on your merry way. What more is there to say? Or is this a social visit? Maybe you wish to revisit our days of yore, when we were teenagers smoking dope behind Santa Fe High and trying desperately to get laid? Yes?"

Fernando frowned. He motioned to the man with the smashed face. "Is that Alhambra, your drug dealer?"

Alhambra stirred in his seat, not liking Fernando's question.

"Yes indeed, that's my assistant, Joey Alhambra," Ziggy said. "Let's cut to the chase, Lopez. What do you want now?"

"I want to know what really happened at the ceremony that night," Fernando fired back. "Mary Logan said you and Chris were fighting before the ceremony even began. Other witnesses said that your pusher friend here had to help Chris to his chair in the fire circle."

"He's not a pusher," Ziggy said.

"He sells fentanyl to old ladies like Mary Logan to keep them addicted," Fernando replied quickly. I call people who sell fentanyl to old ladies swine. What do you call them?"

Alhambra glared at Fernando, a look of pure hatred on his face.

Ziggy shook his head. "Fentanyl is a medicine for pain and anxiety, widely prescribed for those conditions."

"Prescribed by whom? You're not a doctor, Ziggy, you're a cheap, two-bit con man," Fernando said, getting heated now. "Always have been, even back when you were nothing, just a hippie acid freak called Frank Tate."

Now both Alhambra and Ziggy glared at Fernando. "You better leave now, before this gets out of hand," Ziggy said.

"Did you kill Chris Chabot?" Fernando asked suddenly.

Surprised by the question, Ziggy leaned back in his chair and gave Fernando the Evil Eye. "You have a lot of nerve coming in here accusing me of murder. Who the fuck do you think you are? You're not a detective, you're not even a private investigator any more. You're nobody. Now get the fuck out of this office before I have Joey throw you out."

At that Alhambra stood up.

Fernando stared down Alhambra, who stopped in his tracks and made no effort to move forward. "Thing is, Ziggy, no one saw Chris move after Joey carried him to the fire circle. That's because he was already dead. Either you or your drug pusher friend here killed him."

Ziggy shot up, knocking over his chair. "Get out! Get the fuck out of here!" he shouted.

Fernando smiled. "I thought so," he said and walked away.

Fernando stepped outside and walked down the flagstone path to his Cherokee, still smiling. He'd come partly to warn Ziggy about Antonio's threat to come back and "deal" with him. Now he didn't give a damn what Antonio did to Ziggy. Good luck, Ziggy.

Let's see how Ziggy likes a visit from the enforcer.

## 10

After stopping for a green chile cheeseburger at Bobcat Bite, Fernando headed back to Santa Fe. Coming into town on Old Santa Fe Trail, he turned right on the Paseo and took it around to Alameda Street. He always parked on Alameda Street, along the Santa Fe River, when he came downtown. Force of habit. Once he plugged the meter, he walked up Shelby Street and then crossed the Plaza to Washington Avenue. Two blocks down he came to the Washington Avenue Station, where he'd worked for thirty long years.

Inside he found an unfamiliar dispatcher sitting at the front counter, a middle-aged woman with glasses and short blond hair. "Can I help you?" she asked, peering at him over her glasses.

"I'm here to see Manny," Fernando said.

"I'll see if he's in," she said and went to call him.

"No problem, I know where to find him," Fernando said, and walked down the hall to his old office, now Manny's office.

"Hey, Manny," Fernando said, walking into the office.

"Fernando! You coming back to work or what?" Manny asked.

Fernando laughed. "Chief wouldn't approve."

"Yeah, he has me for his whipping boy now," Manny said, pawing through a stack of papers on his desk. "I still can't find a damn thing. I got rid of all your crap, but now mine is starting to pile up. Oh, by the way, we heard from the Medical Examiner in Albuquerque this morning."

Fernando took a seat across from the desk. "Yeah?"

"Turns out Forensics was right," Manny said. "Someone used a wire garrote on Chris and then tried to cover it up by pulling a bolo tie tight around Chris' neck. He died by asphyxiation."

"Caused by the wire?" Fernando asked.

"Well, that's the question now," Manny replied. "The Medical

Examiner's office couldn't tell if the asphyxiation was caused by the wire garrote tightening around the neck or the deep finger indentations around Chris' neck from someone choking him with their hands."

Fernando shook his head, disappointed at the news, because he still didn't know who killed Chris Chabot.

Manny noticed Fernando's dark mood. "What's the matter? You look like someone just shot your dog."

"I just came back from a nasty confrontation with Ziggy and his assistant, Joey Alhambra," Fernando said and then recounted what had happened out at Rancho Nirvana. Who is this guy, Joey Alhambra?"

Manny laughed. "He's been on the radar for years, a nickel and dime drug dealer who does a little business in fentanyl with the Sinaloa Cartel."

"I thought we got rid of the Sinaloa Cartel after the Santa Fe Assassin case," Fernando interrupted.

"We did, but the cartel's still in Albuquerque," Manny said. "They operate in Albuquerque's South Valley, the old barrio. That's Alhambra's connection. Just a short drive away."

Fernando nodded.

"Anyway, Alhambra supplies Ziggy with all the drugs used at Rancho Nirvana, including the peyote for the fire circle ceremonies," Manny said, and then laughed. "Alhambra serves as something of a mini cartel, driving around the Pecos area and even up to some of the old Hispanic villages on the High Road to Taos selling his fucking drugs out of the back of his van, I kid you not. Kind of pathetic."

Fernando laughed too. "Like the old library bookmobile used to be, except he delivers drugs, not books."

"Exactly."

Then Fernando told Manny about his interviews with the three witnesses at the ceremony on the night Chris Chabot was murdered: George Boros, Tom Lujan, and Mary Logan. "All of them said the same thing, that Chris seemed more dead than alive before the ceremony began and that Alhambra had to carry him to his seat."

"Still, that doesn't change the fact that Antonio picked Chris up by the neck and shook him," Antonio said.

"Sure, but it was during an attack of Post Traumatic Stress Syndrome," Fernando responded.

Manny shrugged. "That's not much of a defense in a courtroom. Even the great Raoul Garcia would have a hard time getting an acquittal with that defense. Might get some sympathy from the judge, but not much else."

Fernando frowned. He didn't like the direction their conversation had taken. He decided not to tell Manny about his last conversation with Antonio or that Antonio had decided to come back to Santa Fe and take care of business himself, whatever that meant. Better to keep it on the down-low. Let Antonio contact Manny when he was good and ready.

While they talked, Manny's phone buzzed. Manny picked up the receiver and listened. "No kidding," he said, sitting up straight in his chair. "Okay, I'm on my way, be there in a few."

"I better go," Fernando said.

"Tom Lujan's next door neighbor just found him dead in his house," Manny said, reaching out to Fernando.

"Tom Lujan? He's one of the three witnesses to Chris' death at the peyote ceremony."

"I know," Manny said. "You wanna come? Be like old times."

"Why not?" Fernando replied.

Fernando followed Manny outside to the parking lot and climbed into Manny's cruiser. Unlike everyone else Fernando knew, Manny drove under the speed limit, painfully slow. So slow that it often appeared that he had no idea where he was going or how to get there. Fernando took a deep breath and told himself to relax. He hated riding with Manny.

Oblivious to Fernando's mood, Manny drove slowly to the Paseo and around to Dos Gaspar Avenue, which he took to Coronado Road. At Coronado Road he turned right and drove slowly, traffic honking behind him, one block over to Galisteo Street, where he turned right again and headed back toward downtown.

Fernando could contain himself no longer. "Do you even know where you're going?"

"Sure, it's on Galisteo," Manny said. "Galisteo is a one-way down, Dos Gaspar is a one-way up."

Fernando did not reply.

Halfway down Galisteo Street Manny turned into a short, uphill drive leading to a two-story, gray stone house with a small porch and a pitched roof. Not only that, but the stone house had round windows on the second floor and a cupola on the roof, unusual architecture for Santa Fe. Manny parked behind the Forensics van, which had already arrived.

Fernando stayed back a pace, letting Manny take the lead. They didn't see the Forensics team, Miguel and Teresa, so they walked up to the porch, Fernando a few paces behind. Manny opened the front door and stepped inside. "Hello? Anybody here?" Manny asked.

"We're back here," Miguel said, coming out of what looked like a bedroom down the hall.

Fernando lingered in the front room, which looked like a museum filled with antique furniture: ornate mahogany tables and cabinets and bulky velvet-upholstered chairs and sofas. The front windows, opaque from a layer of dirt, looked like they hadn't been cleaned in months or even years. Dust and cobwebs everywhere. Looked like a room out of a Victorian horror movie. Apparently Tom Lujan did his living in the back rooms.

Joining the others, Fernando noticed an elderly woman talking to Miguel. The woman pointed to a table in the hallway where a covered cooking pot had been placed. "I brought Tom some green chile stew for lunch," the woman said, a stout woman with thick black glasses and braided gray hair. I've been helping take care of him for a while, ever since he found out he needed a liver transplant. I live next door, you know. Judy Romero."

"That's kind of you," Miguel said, a bird-like little man with dark-rimmed glasses and a beak for a nose.

Judy nodded. "I found him like this when I came in. He always leaves the back door open for me."

Miguel moved over to the bed, where Tom Lujan lay on top of a dirty blanket wearing only his jockey shorts. Except for his swollen abdomen, Lujan looked like a scarecrow, his arms and legs nothing but tight skin on bone. Lujan's emaciated face, a sunken pit of deep wrinkles, had taken on the yellowish hue common to people with liver problems.

Manny approached the bed. "Could he have died from liver failure?"

Miguel shrugged. "Possible, but take a look at this. See the tiny feathers on his shoulders and behind his head? If you look closely, there's even a feather in one of his nostrils."

Manny bent over and looked at the feathers. "So?"

"So the only pillow here is down on the floor, not under or near his head," Miguel said.

Fernando stepped closer to take a look. "Are you suggesting Lujan was smothered with the pillow."

"It's possible," Miguel said. "We should know more once we get him down to the lab."

Manny turned to Judy. "You said he left the back door open for you, which means it would have been open for other people. Did you see anyone else enter the house—or anyone hanging around outside?"

Judy shook her head. "No, but I wouldn't. None of my windows overlook his back entrance. It's very private, surrounded by trees."

"What about other cars in his driveway? Did he have any visitors?"

"No, he didn't have any friends or family," Judy said. "His ex-wife died years ago, and they didn't have any children. Rancho Nirvana was about the only place he ever went. I did the shopping for him, whatever he needed. We've been neighbors for over twenty years. I'll miss him."

"That was very kind of you," Manny said. "He was lucky to have such a good neighbor."

Fernando stepped back, away from the bed. Suddenly he found it difficult to breathe. The air was stifling in this shuttered house. He needed fresh air.

"I need to step outside," Fernando said. None of the others paid any attention to him, so he walked out of the bedroom and down the hall to the front door, leaving Manny questioning Judy and Miguel examining the body.

Outside, he shuffled over to the cruiser and climbed into the front passenger's seat, leaving the door open for fresh air. He laid his head back on the head-rest and felt his eyelids grow heavy. He saw dead people everywhere when he closed his eyes. They were waiting for him in his dreams. His nightmares.

## 11

Fernando saw a dim light at the end of a dark hallway. It seemed to be coming from under a door. As he approached he heard the weeping sound again, soft and muffled. Then he heard whispers somewhere in the darkness of the house. The floorboards creaked and groaned as he crept along the wooden floor. He grew more apprehensive the closer he came to the door and the sickly yellow light reaching out to him, drawing him closer. He reached out to grab the doorknob.

"Fernando, wake up," Manny was saying, shaking him by the shoulder. "Damn, you need to get more sleep at night, amigo."

Embarrassed, Fernando tried to shake it off. He took a deep breath and then another. "What's the latest? What does Miguel say?"

"He thinks it's a homicide," Manny said. "Looks like Lujan was smothered with the pillow. We'll know for sure by tomorrow, probably."

Fernando nodded. "So it looks like Ziggy and Joey Alhambra are getting rid of the witnesses."

"Or Antonio," Manny said. "Just like you said. To get rid of witnesses."

"Come on, you don't really think Antonio could have killed Lujan," Fernando replied, getting angry.

Manny shrugged. "All I'm saying is we don't know who's responsible. All of them are suspects, okay?"

But it wasn't okay, not with Fernando. He knew Manny was just doing his job, but he couldn't help feeling that Manny was betraying his friendship with Antonio, one of their best friends.

"Where's your car, I'll drop you off?" Manny asked.

"On Alameda, across from Shelby Street," Fernando said.

Manny climbed into the driver's seat and backed out of the driveway. Then he drove down Galisteo Street to the Paseo and around to Alameda Street. When he stopped beside the Cherokee, he said, "Don't misunderstand, I'm hoping Antonio had nothing to do with either the

Chabot or the Lujan murder, like you. We just have to find out what happened, okay?" He patted Fernando on the back.

Fernando nodded, but said nothing. Instead, he climbed out of the cruiser and watched Manny drive away.

He walked around to his Cherokee and then changed his mind. Instead of heading home, he decided to stop at the La Fonda bar for a cold beer. It had been a long, exhausting day. He hadn't accomplished a damned thing.

Fernando walked up Shelby Street to La Fonda. He avoided the main entrance because he would have to walk by the reception counter, where he might bump into Fred Mondragon, the hotel manager. Fred had banned him from La Fonda for his part in a couple of disturbances involving the so-called Santa Fe Assassin and, most recently, Tom Doering. No matter how many times he'd explained to Fred that he had nothing to do with either disturbance, Fred blamed him for always bringing in a disruptive, lawless class of people. Was it his fault that some of his past clients and their acquaintances were a bit unstable?

So instead of the front door, Fernando went around to the garage entrance and walked down the long hallway to the famous La Fonda Bar. Fortunately the bar was crowded with tourists and other riff-raff, so it should be easy to hide in the crowd. He moved quickly through the tables and up to the bar, where he spotted the familiar figure of Raoul Garcia hunkered down over the bar, head lowered over his margarita. An old friend and sometimes enemy, Raoul was the best damn criminal lawyer in the state of New Mexico.

"Mind if I join you?" Fernando asked, helping himself to the bar stool next to Raoul.

Raoul jumped, spilling his drink. "Lopez—you scared me. I got a lot of enemies, you know."

"Yes, you do," Fernando replied, noticing that Raoul looked even worse than the last time he'd seen him. Wearing a rumpled blue linen blazer and his usual paisley necktie, Raoul's belly bulged out of his open blazer and spilled over his belt. With a bloated face and hands, Raoul looked like a heart attack on two feet. The man was not long for this world.

"Jesus, Raoul, you look like shit," Fernando said.

"Yeah, my fucking cardiologist wants me to have bypass surgery, maybe even a heart transplant," Raoul said, nursing a margarita. "I told him he was crazy, they're not putting me on a table and cutting out my heart. Bunch of fucking witches harvesting body parts!"

Fernando laughed. "Lotta people don't think you have a heart, Raoul."

"What...are you gonna give me a hard time, too?" Raoul asked and then returned to his margarita.

Fernando ordered his usual Modelo draft and studied Raoul, who was no longer the fiery young lawyer Fernando remembered from their youth. Back then Raoul represented radical Chicano leaders and organizations like La Raza as far back as the late eighties. He called his clients "political prisoners," men and women charged with everything from growing pot to making armed raids on county courthouses. Raoul built a reputation for taking on the system every chance he got and winning more times than he lost. Many more times.

Not an easy task for an aggressive, smart-ass Chicano lawyer who all the Anglos in the judicial system hated. But times had changed, and so had Raoul and his clientele. Instead of fire-bombing courthouses, the young apolitical hoodlums he represented now shot each other in gangs over territory or drugs. If not for territory or drugs, then just for the hell of it. And Raoul had changed along with the times. He now did a lucrative business in real estate development and celebrity lawsuits, having become one of the premier trial lawyers in all of northern New Mexico. There wasn't a lawyer or district attorney in the state who didn't fear coming up against Raoul in a courtroom. And for good reason.

Raoul finished his margarita and ordered another. He turned to Fernando. "So another of your friends is in big trouble," he said, out of the blue.

Puzzled, Fernando glanced at Raoul. "How do you know this?"

"He called me," Raoul replied.

"Antonio?"

"Yes, that's what I'm trying to tell you," Raoul said.

"Where is he... in Santa Fe now?" Fernando asked. "I was with him last night in Taos. I just got back this morning."

Raoul shook his head. "You know I can't disclose any information I might have about Antonio. It's lawyer-client privilege."

"So you're defending him. Good," Fernando said. "Just be careful if you go out to Rancho Nirvana. They're not real friendly, I discovered."

Raoul laughed. "Tell me about it. I got that crazy bastard Ziggy off on drug charges more times than I can remember back in the day, before he resurfaced as a fucking therapist, or whatever he calls himself now. He never paid me a cent for any of the work I did for him."

"Who have you talked to so far?" Fernando asked.

"Antonio and Manny," Raoul replied. "Plus I ran into Steve Chabot earlier today. Steve said he kicked Chris out of the house last Spring...that he'd cut off all ties to Chris, who'd been a big disappointment."

"Well, whatever happened during the ceremony the night Chris was murdered is murky," Fernando said. "I think Antonio's being set up to take the fall. I can't prove it, but I think Ziggy and his assistant Joey Alhambra had as much to do with Chris' death as Antonio."

"Yeah...I read the Forensics report," Raoul said, trying to cut off the discussion. "I can't say any more."

## 12

When Fernando walked into their house on Acequia Madre Street, Estelle was in the kitchen making his favorite meal: cheese enchiladas with red chile and posole. She admitted to feeling bad about their recent argument and said she wanted to make up for her part in the argument. "But first, at least tell me where and what you're doing whenever you leave, so I know where to look for you in case you disappear," she joked. Sort of.

Fernando told her about what had happened at the peyote ceremony at Rancho Nirvana and that at the moment Antonio was the number one suspect in the murder of Chris Chabot. "So I'm just trying to help Antonio prove his innocence," Fernando explained.

Estelle shook her head. "Why would Antonio murder Chris Chabot? I don't understand."

"Well, his Post Traumatic Stress Disorder has returned," Fernando said. "Witnesses claim he went crazy and strangled Chabot, but I don't think that's what happened. I think Chabot was already dead when Antonio grabbed him."

Estelle stared at him from across the kitchen. "Then who did kill Chabot?"

Fernando shrugged. "I don't know yet."

"And why is Antonio participating in this peyote circle?" Estelle asked. "To treat his Post Traumatic Stress Disorder?"

"Exactly," Fernando replied. "It's supposed to draw participants out of their anxiety or depression, whatever's bothering them. Apparently the intense visions, the distortions of time and space, and the detachment from self, all aid in the recovery process. Or so I'm told."

"Whatever you say," Estelle said, sounding doubtful.

Over dinner Fernando described the peyote ceremony from the

beginning when the road chief who conducts the ceremony passes around a bag of peyote to the final water call. The participants eat as many of the dried peyote buttons as they want and then talk about themselves and what they're seeing in their visions. Sometimes they sing or chant along with the road chief, who takes them down peyote road. The ceremony usually ends at Midnight or the next morning.

Estelle listened, but said nothing. It was clear she had no interest in hearing more. Which suited Fernando just fine, because he had no interest in dwelling on the murky subject.

That night he had the best sleep he'd had in weeks. No nightmare about being trapped in a dark house with a woman sobbing in a room down a long, dark hallway. Instead, he dreamed of the times he'd climbed Santa Fe Baldy with his late friend Fidel Rodriguez and his missing friend Antonio Blake. Hiking to the top of Baldy where they sat on the pinnacle drinking wine or beers from their backpacks. Good times with good friends.

He slept until almost 9 a.m., late for him. He felt great, better than he had in a long time. He looked around for Estelle, but then realized she'd left for work over an hour ago. He dressed quickly and went to the kitchen, thinking about breakfast. Hoping to find leftovers he could eat quickly, he checked in the refrigerator but found nothing. So he poured himself a bowl of Estelle's granola and brewed himself a cup of coffee in the Keurig coffeemaker. He took everything outside to the patio and sat on the bench overlooking Estelle's flower garden. He sipped his coffee slowly trying to work up an appetite for the cold granola, which he didn't particularly like, even though Estelle claimed it was healthier than the leftovers he usually ate.

Before he could get himself to try the granola, his cell phone rang inside the house. He'd left it on the kitchen counter. He hurried inside and clicked the accept button.

"Fernando, I'm told Antonio's in town somewhere," Manny said. "Do you know where?"

"News to me," Fernando said after a long pause, although it wasn't really news. "Who told you this?"

"Your favorite lawyer, Raoul Garcia," Manny said. "He called me this morning and said Antonio had hired him. Said I better have some damn good physical evidence before arresting Antonio. Threatened to have me fired if I didn't. Same old Raoul, bullying and threatening to get his way."

"He's right, though," Fernando said. "The district attorney will need more than circumstantial evidence if he goes up against Raoul Garcia, especially trying to convict a former cop."

Manny sighed. "I know, Fernando, but at this point I'm just trying to question Antonio, not arrest him, okay? The Chief's after my ass, as usual. You remember the Chief, right?"

"I remember all too well," Fernando replied. "I'm trying to find Antonio the same as you. If I find him, I'll let you know."

"Bullshit!" Manny said and clicked off.

Fernando went back outside and finished his coffee. He sat on the bench thinking about Antonio. If Antonio had come back to Santa Fe, as seemed likely based on what Manny said, then where would he be staying? Fernando knew Antonio kept camping gear in his Wrangler so that he could camp off-road any time he wanted. Problem was, there must be dozens, if not hundreds, of unmarked forest roads in the Santa Fe area, which included the Sangre de Cristo Mountains as well as the Pecos Wilderness area. Finding Antonio would be like finding the proverbial needle in a haystack. The Pecos seemed more likely simply because Antonio lived there and knew the area like the back of his hand.

When he finished brooding, he stared at his cold, coagulating granola. Can't do it, he decided. He took the bowl back inside and dumped the granola in the trash. This morning he needed a good, substantial breakfast burrito.

Fernando locked the house and climbed into his Cherokee. Driving down to the Paseo, he swung around to Cerrillos Road and drove straight to Café Castro, one of his favorites. He knew their breakfast burrito was tops. The only burrito that came close was the Sagebrush Inn's breakfast burrito, but that was in Taos.

He pulled into the Café Castro parking lot, which was nearly empty given the awkward hour, between breakfast and lunch. Inside, the small round tables were all empty, so he walked up to the counter and ordered his breakfast burrito to go. Alice, the server, took his order and came back with the burrito a few minutes later. He took his order out to the Cherokee and drove back around to Alameda Street, parking along the Santa Fe River.

Hungry, he took his food to a picnic table beside the river and devoured the burrito quickly. He wished he'd ordered a drink, because the chile was hot this morning and he needed something to wash down the food. His bad. Then he remembered he kept a six-pack of bottled water in the rear compartment of the Cherokee. He grabbed one of the plastic bottles when he got ready to leave, leaning against the Cherokee as he drank down half of the bottle.

While he drank his water, Fernando considered what to do next. He had no idea where to look for Antonio. He would have to wait until Noon when Antonio was supposed to call. Meanwhile, why not check out Chris Chabot's apartment? Maybe he could figure out who might want to kill Chabot by searching his apartment. Ruby mentioned that Chabot lived at Fort Marcy Apartments, where Chabot's father paid the rent. He checked the address online and found Chabot listed at Number 12, Fort Marcy Apartments.

Fernando was all too familiar with Fort Marcy Apartments—an old, slightly rundown complex that resembled a two-story Marriott Residence Inn without the charm. Fort Marcy Apartments catered to younger, less-affluent renters than most other apartments in Santa Fe. During his years as a police detective he'd been called there on several occasions, most involving domestic abuse or drug-related issues. A bit shady, that's how he remembered the place.

Determined, he climbed into his Cherokee and drove up to the Paseo and over to Bishop's Lodge Road. Once past the turn-off to Hyde Park Road, Fort Marcy Apartments came into view. Clearly the apartments had been spiffed up since his days on the Santa Fe Police Department. The units had been newly painted and the landscape gardening had been improved with the addition of bright flowers and bushes all around the compound. Even a new sign, which advertised a vacancy.

Fernando pulled up in front of Number 12, one of the units on the lower level of the frame and stucco building. Wooden stairways led to the rooms on the upper level. No one happened to be around, so he moseyed over to the door of Number 12 and tried the door knob. Locked, as expected. So he took out his lock pick and helped himself. Once inside the dark efficiency, he groped around on the wall trying to find a light switch. When he did, he clicked the switch but nothing happened. No electricity. PNM had turned off Chabot's electricity.

Fernando took out his cell phone and clicked on its flashlight app. The weak splash of light revealed a tiny efficiency apartment with an open floor plan. On the right side he saw a kitchen counter separating the front sitting room from the kitchen. To the left he saw a tiny bedroom and bath. Clutter of one kind or another literally buried the scant furniture and kitchen counter. Dirty dishes, fast food wrappers, old newspapers, and assorted trash covered everything. An overflowing garbage can had been moved to the center of the kitchen floor, as if Chabot had started to take out the garbage and then stopped for some reason. The place was a goddamn pigpen.

Making his way to the kitchen counter he avoided stepping on piles of trash, including empty beer cans and bottles. On the kitchen counter he found a pile of bills, most of them overdue, spread out on the tiles.

The PNM bill, the water and gas bills, even an overdraft statement from the First National Bank of Santa Fe. Clearly, Chris Chabot had a money problem.

From there Fernando shuffled around the counter and glanced into the bedroom, where dirty clothes and blankets smothered a single bed. The stench coming from the room dissuaded him from entering. Instead, he walked over to the kitchen table where he found a small plastic bag of fentanyl. Only three of the blue pills remained, along with a pinch of blue fentanyl dust.

No surprise there. All Doctor Ziggy's clients at Rancho Nirvana had drug problems, mostly fentanyl. The national drug of choice, it seemed.

Fernando turned around and headed back to the front door, eager to get out of the dirty, cramped space. He clicked off the flashlight app when he came to the door. On his way out the door he encountered a pudgy, middle-aged man wearing a bright blue suit with a bright red bowtie.

Fernando did a double-take. You didn't see many bowties in Santa Fe.

"Hey, what are you going in Chris Chabot's apartment?" the middle-aged man asked.

"PNM collections," Fernando shot back, without thinking. "Chabot is behind on his bills. We had to turn off his electricity last week. We're checking to see if he still lives here."

The man shook his head. "I wouldn't doubt it. He's strung out on dope. He begs money from everyone here. Good luck catching up with him."

"Thanks," Fernando said, watching the man walk to his car, an old Buick convertible with dented fenders.

He watched the Buick drive out of the parking lot and turn left toward Santa Fe. He took a deep breath. Fresh air never smelled so fragrant.

# 13

Fernando sat at his kitchen table staring at his cell phone. The screen read 12:35. Antonio was more than a half-hour late on his daily call. Why? In his mind Fernando went over all the terrible things that could have befallen Antonio. He'd almost convinced himself that he would never hear from his friend again when his cell phone began ringing and dancing on the table top.

"You're late," Fernando answered.

"Just got back from a long hike," Antonio said.

"Where are you?" Fernando asked. "I hear you've been talking to Raoul Garcia. He said you were back in Santa Fe."

"Yeah, I'm back at my cabin," Antonio said, without explanation.

"You're not worried they'll find you?"

"No, I parked my Wrangler over on the forest road that runs parallel to my drive," Antonio said. "If I see a vehicle coming up the drive, I'll duck out my back door and run up the mountain. They'll never find me."

"Okay...then stay put, I'll be there in thirty minutes, we need to talk," Fernando said, clicking off.

Fernando wasted no time. He quickly locked up the house and raced down to the Paseo and over to the Old Santa Fe Trail, which slowed him down to a crawl because of all the tourists coming from or going to Interstate 25. He sped up again when the road merged with the Old Las Vegas Highway. The Santa Fe suburbs fell away as the landscape changed to green forest and rolling hills.

Just before the town of Pecos Fernando turned off on the forest road that would take him to Antonio's long driveway. To his right, further up in altitude, he could almost see the forest road that paralleled Antonio's driveway, where Antonio had parked his Wrangler. This ridge was where the killer called the Foreman from the Pecos Reckoning case fired down on them. Bad memories. Antonio had been seriously wounded in that shoot-out.

He drove slowly over the rough road, still cratered with ruts and jutting rocks after its latest grading. As expected, he didn't see Antonio's wrangler as he approached the rustic log cabin under the tall Ponderosa pines.

What he did see pissed him off. In front of the cabin Antonio sat in one of two folding camp chairs with an Igloo cooler at his feet and a can of beer in his right hand. Here he was racing around as if possessed, trying to help Antonio clear his name, while Antonio was sipping a cold beer and looking as relaxed as Fernando had ever seen him. Didn't the man realize the gravity of his situation.

Fernando slammed the door of the Cherokee and walked to the cabin.

Antonio glanced at his watch. "You're five minutes later than I thought you'd be. You're slowing down, amigo."

"Hah!" Fernando shot back. "I've been racing around trying to find out who killed Christ Chabot. What have you been doing?"

"I've been sitting here waiting for you," Antonio said.

Then Fernando noticed Antonio was drinking a Modelo Especial. "Well, at least you have good taste in beer."

"I bought that for you," Antonio said. "To me, it tastes like cat piss. I usually drink something stronger. An ale or a stout."

Fernando sat down in the other camp chair and helped himself to a can of Modelo. "So why did you decide to come back now?"

"Because I didn't kill Chris Chabot," Antonio said. "In Taos, after you left, I went out to Arroyo Seco to visit an old Marine buddy who teaches deep meditation. He guided me through a session. I revisited what happened that night at Rancho Nirvana and saw for myself. I might have grabbed Chris by the neck and shaken him, but only because I was trying to get his attention...to wake him up...but I couldn't. Meditating, I saw clearly that I didn't kill him."

"No, because he was already dead when Alhambra brought him out to the peyote circle," Fernando agreed. "At least that's what I think happened."

"Then the question is: who really killed Chris?" Antonio added.

Fernando took a long drink from his Modelo and shook his head. "Good question. Ziggy or his so-called assistant Alhambra, I suppose. They were both fighting with Chris before the ceremony."

"Don't forget George Boros," Antonio replied. "He and Chris fought all the time. George had a grudge against Chris, who'd borrowed money from him and never paid it back. Something like that."

"News to me," Fernando said.

Suddenly Antonio pointed to the forest road about a quarter mile away, where a black Escalade was approaching his driveway.

"Here they come," Antonio said, standing up and finishing his can of Modelo. He tossed the empty can in the Igloo cooler and said, "You take care of this. I'll be on the mountain behind the house."

"My pleasure," Fernando said.

While Antonio went into the cabin and out the back door to the trail that led to the top of the mountain, Fernando watched the Escalade turn into Antonio's driveway and slowly make its way up the rough road. It looked like the same Escalade he'd seen at Rancho Nirvana. No surprise there.

Fernando waited patiently for the big, unwieldy vehicle to bounce its way up the driveway. Finally it pulled in behind his Cherokee and stalled. Both front doors opened and two men jumped out. The driver was Alhambra with the flat face, wearing a slick black exercise suit. The passenger looked much older, a scrawny, asthmatic man with a cough who he'd never seen before. The scrawny man appeared strung out. Nervous, even skittish.

Fernando raised his can of Modelo as if to greet them. He noticed both of them wore open carry holsters.

"What are you doing here?" Alhambra barked. His mouth barely moved when he spoke, squashed flat like the rest of his face.

"The same thing you're doing, looking for Antonio," Fernando responded, realizing that Alhambra's smashed face looked like the face of a Bull Dog.

Alhambra frowned, suspicious. "Then why are you sitting there drinking by yourself?"

"Why not? You got something better to do?" Fernando shot back.

"Listen, I don't know who you are or what you're doing here, but you need to keep your nose out of Doctor Ziggy's business," Alhambra said, snarling. "That means staying away from Rancho Nirvana and staying away from his clients, the people who attend his ceremonies."

"You mean the people you sell fentanyl to," Fernando said.

The scrawny older man coughed. "You want me to take care of him?" he asked Alhambra, reaching for his pistol.

"No!" Joey barked. "Let me take care of this."

Fernando smiled. "Yeah, calm down," he said to the scrawny man and reached into the Igloo cooler for another can of Modelo. He held out the can of beer to Alhambra. "Have a beer, why don't you?"

The coughing man hissed, like a fucking snake.

"Or do you prefer fentanyl?" Fernando asked.

"Don't press your luck, old timer," Alhambra snapped. He turned to his companion. "Go check out the cabin."

When the coughing man went into the cabin, Alhambra sat down in the second camp chair and took the can of Modelo from Fernando. He popped the top and took a drink.

"Good," Fernando said. "Hell, maybe we can even become friends."

Alhambra looked askance at Fernando and then asked, "Ziggy says you used to be a cop...that right?"

Fernando nodded. "And so did Antonio. They called him the 'enforcer' down at the station."

"I can imagine, he's a big motherfucker," Alhambra replied. He tipped back his head and drained half the can of Modelo. Moments later he tipped his head back again and drank the second half of the Modelo. Dropping the can in the Igloo, he turned to Fernando. "So what do you call yourself now?"

"I call myself a fixer," Fernando said.

"A fixer? What do you fix?"

"Whatever needs fixing," Fernando said. "I clean up other people's messes by whatever means necessary."

"And you think what happened during the ceremony at Rancho Nirvana was a mess? Who's mess?" Alhambra asked.

Fernando smiled. "That remains to be seen, doesn't it?"

Just then coughing man came out of the cabin. "No sign of him in the cabin," he reported, wheezing badly.

Alhambra nodded and stood up. He walked to the Escalade and then turned back to Fernando. "We'll be back."

"I don't doubt it," Fernando replied.

Watching the black Escalade drive off slowly, as solemn as a hearse, Fernando made a mental note to start wearing his Smith & Wesson again. Alhambra could be a problem.

# 14

On the way back to Santa Fe Fernando stopped at Bobcat Bite's parking lot. He took out his cell phone and searched for George Boros' home address. He found it on East Bueno Vista Street, right off Old Santa Fe Trail. The news that Boros and Chris Chabot had been involved in a heated argument immediately before the ceremony in which Chabot was murdered raised other questions, other possibilities in the quest to find Chabot's murderer. He intended to find out more about this argument between Boros and Chris Chabot.

He pulled out on the Old Las Vegas Highway and took it into Santa Fe. Once past Coronado Road he knew he was getting closer. The second left turned out to be East Buena Vista. He made the left turn and slowed down, looking for the right address. He found it mid-block, a single-story faux adobe, looked like cinder block, with a flat roof and a wrought iron fence surrounding the front yard. Not much to look at, except maybe the hollyhock and sunflower garden that provided red and yellow color to an otherwise bland property.

Parking on the street, Fernando climbed out of the Cherokee and walked up to the gate. Fortunately the gate wasn't locked, so he made his way through the flowers up to a cement slab porch and rang the bell. When no one answered, he rang the bell again and knocked on the wooden door. Moments later the door opened, revealing a middle-aged woman wearing a yellow cotton dress. She did not look happy to have a visitor. She stared at him through gray-streaked auburn bangs, which almost distracted him from noticing her black eye. Black and purple would be more accurate. In fact, the right side of her face looked swollen, as if someone had used her as a punching bag. Fernando didn't have a hard time guessing who.

'Yes...?' the woman said tentatively.

"Sorry to bother you," Fernando started, "but I'm here to see George about what happened the other night at Rancho Nirvana. Is he home?"

She shook her head. "No, we're separated. He's staying at the Residence Inn up the street. The one at Galisteo and Saint Michael's Drive."

Fernando knew the place well. He'd had more than one client staying there over the years. Not a bad place to stay temporarily if your wife kicked you out of the house for domestic abuse.

He noticed the woman's hands were noticeably shaking. "Are you okay, Mrs. Boros?"

A lone tear ran down her left cheek. She shook her head. "No, not really."

Fernando motioned toward her eye. "Did your husband do that to you?"

"Of course, who else?" she replied quickly.

Fernando did not like what he was hearing. He prided himself on physically punishing women abusers however and whenever he could, delivering much-deserved ass-whippings to the men he considered the lowest scum of the earth. He smiled when he thought of how he and Antonio used to deal with women beaters. On more than one occasion he had to step in and prevent Antonio from killing the unfortunate miscreant who fell into Antonio's huge hands. Antonio prided himself on never touching his ex-wife, even while experiencing severe Post Traumatic Stress Syndrome.

"I'm very sorry, Mrs. Boros," Fernando said. "I had no idea that your husband was a domestic abuser."

She lowered her eyes. "He has a bad temper. Sometimes he can't control it and he does some bad things."

"I understand," Fernando said, "but you need to distance yourself from him. I would get a restraining order so he can't just show up here one day and try to hit you again."

She nodded, sniffling now.

Fernando took a business card out of his shirt pocket. "Here, take my card. If he ever tries to lay a hand on you again, call me. I'll take care of him. Really, it will be my pleasure."

She nodded.

"By the way, what's your first name?" Fernando asked.

"Angela," she said.

"Nice name," Fernando replied. "I'll be in touch...Angela."

He walked back to the Cherokee and climbed inside. He headed to the Residence Inn at the corner of Galisteo and Saint Michael's Drive. His aversion to men abusing women ran deep in his psyche, back to his childhood. He'd seen his father hit his mother twice and stepped in to help. The first time, at the age of eight or nine, he yelled at his father and tried to throw a punch himself, but his father just laughed and pushed him away with his hand on Fernando's head. The second time, when he was a teenager of eighteen, with his full adult weight of one hundred and eighty pounds, all muscle from playing sports and lifting weights, he stepped in and hit his father so hard the old man flew up in the air and landed flat on his back. The old man never hit his mother again, as far as he knew.

Approaching the Residence Inn on Galisteo, he turned into the drive and stopped at the office. He spotted a young woman inside at the front counter, so he put on his 'Good Time Charlie' face and stepped through the door. "Hi there, just got a call from an old friend of mine, George Boros, who's staying here," Fernando said. "I forgot to get his room number. We're gonna hit up the town this afternoon and all night long. He's a real party animal!"

The young woman smiled, probably because to her he was an old timer and hardly looked like a party animal. She paused for a moment and then went to her computer and hit a few keys. "George Boros, he's in room two fifteen," she said, flashing him another awkward smile. "Don't overdo it, now. Or you know what they say, you'll pay the piper tomorrow."

Fernando winked. "We'll try to keep it legal."

The young woman laughed as he walked out of the office. He climbed into the Cherokee and drove around behind the Residence Inn until he found the rooms in the two hundreds. Then he pulled over in front of a wooden stairway leading to the second floor. He climbed the stairs slowly, making sure not to make too much noise. Didn't want to scare Boros. He had something else in mind.

When he came to Room 215, toward the middle of the walkway, he banged on the door hard and kept banging until the door flew open and a sleepy, disoriented George Boros appeared in the doorway wearing chinos and a plaid shirt with shirttails hanging loose. Must have been sleeping.

"What...what do you want?" Boros asked, stroking his unshaven face. He looked tired and haggard.

"I need to ask you a couple more questions about what happened at the peyote ceremony the night Chris Chabot was killed at Rancho Nirvana," Fernando replied, stepping forward.

"Okay, but who told you where I was staying?" Boros asked, trying to stand his ground.

Fernando brushed past Boros and then turned to face the bewildered man. "Your wife. Did you give her the black eye?"

"Figures, the bitch—"

Fernando moved with lightning speed. He grabbed Boros by the shirt collar and smashed him back into the flimsy wall, which shook as though it were about to come crashing down on them. "You lay a hand on her again and it'll be the last time you ever touch a woman!" he spit in Boros' face. Then he spun Boros around and shoved him as hard as he could.

Crashing against a heavy bureau, Boros yelped and immediately grabbed his shoulder. He sank down on the carpeted floor cursing. "Owww...you fucker...you hurt my shoulder."

Fernando snarled at Boros. "That's not the only thing I'm going to hurt. So you and Chris Chabot got into a fight right before the ceremony—it wasn't just an argument. Right?"

"No!" Boros roared. "We argued about the money he owed me...and when I insisted he pay it, he shoved me away...and then I shoved him back, away from me. That's all that happened. I swear, goddamnit!"

Fernando stared at Boros, weighing what the man had just said.

"I'm telling you the truth," Boros pleaded. "We just shoved each other a little bit—we didn't actually fight. Who told you we got into a fight? They're lying. Now please, leave me alone!"

Fernando nodded, still not certain he believed Boros. Finally he turned to walk away and then stopped. He pointed at Boros and said, "I gave your wife my card. Remember what I said."

With that, Fernando stepped outside and slammed the door.

15

Revved up, riding a burst of adrenaline, Fernando decided to show up for Happy Hour at El Farol this afternoon. He hadn't made it to Happy Hour for the last few days. He drove down Galisteo to the Paseo and around to Canyon Road, parking in the lot across from El Farol. Walking across Canyon Road he spotted Ruby coming down the sidewalk from her gallery.

"'Bout time you showed up," Ruby said. "I was beginning to think you were on the wagon."

Fernando laughed. "No way."

"Did you find Antonio?" Ruby asked, walking up to join him.

"Yeah, but I still don't know what exactly transpired at the peyote ceremony the night Chris was murdered," Fernando said. "Lotta versions of arguments, pushing and shoving, that kind of stuff before the ceremony even began. I don't trust any of the accounts. Not completely, anyway."

They climbed the steps to the La Fonda porch. "Well, I think Manny's being a real prick for not trusting Antonio," Ruby said.

"I know, but he's just doing his job," Fernando replied.

As soon as they opened the door they heard Blaine Rogers' loud, obnoxious voice bellowing in the restaurant part of El Farol. "Hell no, you can't have any more space in my gallery."

"Fuck you, Blaine, you said it was our gallery now," responded Tessa Montez, Ruby's younger sister, who'd closed her gallery in Abiquiu and moved herself and her stock to Santa Fe to share Blaine's Canyon Road gallery, Picasso and Co. "All I need is one more wall."

Their on-again, off-again relationship had been driving everyone around them crazy. They fought nonstop, which puzzled all their friends, because they also talked nonstop about getting married, or 'hitched' as Blaine referred to marriage. Blaine was about as sensitive as a stone.

"Oh for Chrissake Tess, you should have left most of that shit up in Abiquiu," Blaine said. "This is Canyon Road in Santa Fe! We don't sell that cheap crap down here."

"Big fucking deal," Tessa replied. "You haven't sold anything in weeks!"

Hearing them argue, Ruby stomped into the dining area and told them to shut up in no uncertain terms: "Shut up! You're gonna get us all thrown out of here...like you usually do!"

Tessa gave Blaine the finger. "That's it. I can't talk to him any more, I'm moving out," she said to Ruby.

"Go..." Blaine said, leaning back in his chair, hands behind his head.

Across the table from Blaine and Tessa sat old Dave Stein, pushing 90, wearing the same blue suit he'd worn for the past twenty years. With a bald head and tufts of gray hair coming out of his ears, Dave didn't hear very well. He kept asking what? What'd they say?" speaking out of the corner of his mouth, like he was a ventriloquist without a dummy.

"Oh, just ignore these two assholes," Ruby said to Fernando, taking a seat at the table next to Tessa.

Meanwhile, sitting a ways back from the table, Paul and June Bryan sat by themselves and whispered to each other. The Bryans owned Essentia, the sex shop next to Ruby's Gallery. Very proper and very boring, they rarely made an appearance at Happy Hour.

"What's the occasion? I rarely see you two here?" Ruby asked the Bryans.

"Bored," Paul answered.

"We finally hired a part-time clerk to spell us," June said, a tiny young woman with blue hair wearing a skimpy yoga leotard that made her look half naked. June was a licensed masseuse and yoga instructor, both of which she practiced—and occasionally taught—in one of the back rooms at Essentia. What else she practiced there was nobody's business.

Fernando smiled, sitting down next to Ruby. Every time he'd seen June, she'd been wearing a skimpy leotard. He wondered if she ever took off the leotard. To sleep? To have sex?

Penny, one of the newer bartenders, brought Ruby her usual margarita and Fernando his usual Modelo draft. Everyone who worked at El Farol knew what Ruby and Fernando drank.

"We've got bigger problems," Ruby said.

Everyone at the table looked at Ruby.

"Antonio's missing...or in hiding, rather," Ruby said.

Blaine brushed Tessa hands away. "What's this all about?"

Fernando explained the situation: that Antonio was the number one suspect in the murder of Chris Chabot during a peyote ceremony at Doctor Ziggy's Rancho Nirvana; and that so far Manny had ignored other possible suspects including Doctor Ziggy, Doctor Ziggy's man Joey Alhambra, and maybe even George Boros, who had a history of domestic violence.

Blaine shook his head. "Yeah, Ziggy's lost it. He used to be the Santa Fe version of Ken Kesey, driving that psychedelic school bus around town with all the half-naked teenage women inside. The counterculture, what a time it was! Hell, I can't say I was much different."

Ruby guffawed. "You can say that again. Still aren't."

Blaine gave Ruby a dirty look and continued. "Now Ziggy's turned into a fucking drug dealer. He's the candy man of Apache Canyon. Instead of LSD, he and his boy Alhambra now sell mostly fentanyl and meth. I used to buy a lot of weed from them before weed became legal in New Mexico, but I threw their asses out the last time they stopped by my gallery when they tried to sell me fentanyl. Fucking fentanyl! As if I wanted or needed a downer."

Ruby smiled. "I don't know, Blaine, you get pretty worked up. You might need something to calm your nerves."

"Hah! That shit puts you in a coma!" Blaine replied.

Ruby laughed. "Yeah, I took an opioid after a wisdom tooth extraction and passed out dead to the world. I found myself on my hands and knees slobbering on the floor. No thank you. Give me a margarita and a few tokes of weed."

Fernando tried to change the subject from the days of wine and roses, or in this case margaritas and weed, to the murder of Chris Chabot. "So what do you think of this Alhambra character? Is he violent?"

Blaine coughed. "Yeah...he's Ziggy's muscle, what do you think?"

"Why, did he threaten you?"

"Look at me," Blaine said, exasperated. "You think that little prick would threaten me?"

Fernando laughed. "No, I guess not."

Not only was Blaine almost as huge as Antonio at six feet, five inches and two hundred and fifty pounds, he had a nasty temper and went ballistic when angry, just like Antonio. Not to mention that Blaine was handy with the Glock 9 mm. he kept in his office, thanks to his years in the military. Fernando had seen Blaine in action several times. If Alhambra tried to strong-arm Blaine, Alhambra would get a beat down he wouldn't forget.

"Have you noticed Alhambra's face looks smashed, like someone took a two-by-four and smacked him in the face?" Blaine asked.

Fernando nodded.

"Well, if he messes with me, he'll look a lot worse than that," Blaine added. "So if this guy gives you a problem, give me a call and I'll be happy to take care of him. My pleasure."

Fernando checked his watch. "I just might do that."

"Owww, get your hands off me," Tessa snapped at Blaine, changing the topic at the table. Tessa and Blaine started arguing again. Soon the Bryans snuck off, followed by Dave Stein.

Ruby shook her head. "For them, marriage is like mortal combat. The one who survives gets the spoils."

Fernando smiled. He finished his Modelo and then followed Dave Stein, sneaking out of El Farol before either of the love/hate birds could notice him.

Ruby watched him leave, looking downright abandoned.

## 16

Fernando opened the door slowly. The dim light from within grew brighter as he opened the door. What he saw looked suspiciously like the parlor of his grandmother's house back in the 1950s. Dark rugs on the floor, dark wallpaper on the wall, and dark drapes smothering the windows. On the massive mahogany bureau off to the side two yellow candles flickered and danced shadows on the wall. He smelled it now, the odor of closure and stagnation and dust so thick you could barely breath. He grabbed his throat and then took out the bandana he always kept in his rear pocket and placed it over his face like a mask. He heard it again, the soft, liquid sound of someone weeping in the next room.

"Fernando? Fernando?" a voice was calling, drawing him to the surface of consciousness. He opened his eyes to find Estelle leaning over him. She did not look happy.

"I'm just now leaving for work," Estelle said. "Manny has called twice this morning. He wants you to call him right away."

"Mmm...." Fernando managed to mutter, searching for words.

"So call him back, okay?" Estelle said. "I should be home no later than five o'clock."

Fernando struggled to sit up in bed. He watched Estelle walk out of their bedroom and down the hall to the kitchen. Then he heard the kitchen door open and close, followed by the sound of Estelle's Camry starting and driving down the driveway to Acequia Madre Street.

He checked the time. Nearly nine o'clock. Once again. For some reason he'd been sleeping later than usual. He'd become a prisoner of his dreams. He couldn't seem to shake the dream about finding his way out of the dark house. Why? What did it signify, if anything? He had no idea.

Starting to wake up, he climbed out of bed and went into the bathroom to do his business. Then he dressed and made his way to the kitchen, still groggy. Fortunately, Estelle had left him a half pot of coffee, so he poured himself a cup and looked around for his cell phone, which he had somehow misplaced. He found it finally in his study, where he must have placed it after returning from El Farol yesterday. He took the phone and a cup of coffee out to the patio, where he liked to start his day. After a few drinks of coffee, he set the cup on the bench beside him and dialed Manny.

"Fernando, I've been trying to reach you all morning," Manny answered.

"So I hear," Fernando managed to get in before Manny continued.

"Steve Chabot called first thing this morning," Manny said. "He wants to meet with me and Raoul Garcia today at eleven o'clock in my office. Apparently he has evidence to share with us, something he found on Chris' computer. He wants Raoul to be involved because Raoul's defending Antonio, our primary suspect. Can you come? I'd like you to be there to hear what Steve has to say. I know you're investigating on your own, trying to help Antonio."

Surprised, Fernando took a long moment to respond. "I guess, if you think it's appropriate. What do you suppose he's found?"

"Sounds like something in Chris' e-mail," Manny said. "He wouldn't be more specific."

"Okay, I'll be there," Fernando said and clicked off.

Eleven o'clock didn't give him much time to put on his game face. He was a bit apprehensive about this meeting. He and Steve Chabot didn't like each other much, never had. The bad blood between them dated to the early two thousands when Chabot questioned his investigation in a high-profile murder case involving the owner of a gallery on the Santa Fe Plaza. In that and other high-profile cases Chabot criticized his methods, claiming Fernando too often went outside official—that is, legal—practices. What Chabot refused to understand was that sometimes you had to bend the rules a bit in order to get results.

That, in essence, was where the two of them differed. Chabot stressed methods, Fernando stressed results.

Fernando went back inside the kitchen for another cup of coffee. He couldn't seem to get enough coffee these days. It took him several cups to overcome the groggy, underwater feeling that greeted him every morning when he first opened his eyes. The recurring dream didn't help.

This time he took his cup of coffee and his *Santa Fe Independent* into his study. His routine was to read the morning newspaper every morning while he drank his coffee. Today's update in the ongoing Chris Chabot murder story mentioned the suspicious death of Tom Lujan. The update ended with a short paragraph stating that Chief Detective Manny Alvarez was scheduled to hold a press conference to answer questions about the Chabot murder at three o'clock this afternoon.

That confused Fernando. Manny had not mentioned any breakthroughs in the case, or anything new to report. Maybe what came out of the meeting with Steve Chabot would be the news.

He brooded on what Steve Chabot might have to say about his son Chris until a quarter to eleven. Then he headed out the kitchen door, only to stop halfway out and come back inside. He walked into his study and took his Smith & Wesson out of the closet, strapping on its open carry holster. Then, finally, he was ready.

For the first time in days, Fernando would be armed and ready. For what he didn't know. Yet.

## 17

The damn tourists had taken all his usual parking spaces on Alameda Street along the Santa Fe River, so Fernando had to drive around the Paseo to Marcy Street and park near the offices of the *Santa Fe Independent*. He fed the meter and walked down to the rear door of the Washington Avenue Station. Inside he made his way through the labyrinthine building to the main hallway, where Manny's office door was closed. He knocked and waited for Manny to respond.

"It's open," came from inside the room, Manny's voice.

Fernando opened the door to find Manny sitting at his desk looking across at Steve Chabot and Raoul Garcia. Chabot, a tight-ass, wore his usual three-piece suit with necktie pulled tight around his scrawny neck. The tall, thin Chabot with a shock of black hair falling across his forehead looked like a mannequin specifically designed to resemble an anal-retentive prick.

Raoul, on the other hand, was a rumpled mess this morning. His garish purple suit looked like it hadn't been ironed in years. He had the sleeves of the jacket pushed up past his elbows and his shirt collar unbuttoned to the middle of his chest. He seemed dangerously overheated, with sweat beading on his face and slithering down his fat neck. Seriously overweight, Raoul also looked seriously ill.

"Lopez...I didn't know you would be here," Chabot said in his usual icy tone.

"I invited him," Manny said.

Fernando flashed Chabot a mock salute and then sat in a chair off to the side of the desk, giving him a view of all three participants.

"Well, let's get started then," Chabot said. "I have two pieces of information for you. First, I will recuse myself from this case involving my son if and when it moves forward, for obvious reasons. Jim Patterson, the Assistant District Attorney, has agreed to prosecute the case."

Manny nodded, fully expecting Chabot to step away from the case. Not much news there.

"Second, in the pursuit of justice, I wanted to share with you something I found on my son's computer," Chabot continued. "I'm talking about an e-mail exchange back and forth between my son and this so-called Doctor Ziggy. To make a long story short, my son was trying to blackmail Ziggy. It seems that Chris had a fentanyl addiction and had gone deep in debt buying fentanyl and peyote from Ziggy. Chris, unfortunately, never paid his bills, so I'm not terribly surprised by this. Ziggy wanted Chris to ask me for the money to pay his drug bills, but Chris knew I would say no and again send him to rehab. So instead, Chris decided to blackmail Ziggy. He threatened to expose Ziggy and his associate Joey Alhambra's drug business selling fentanyl, amphetamines, and I guess some other psychedelic drugs. The e-mail exchange ends with Ziggy telling Chris to watch his step, that he was skating on thin ice. In other words, that his life was in danger."

"Wow!" Manny said. "And you have the actual e-mails?"

"Yes, I will make you and Counselor Garcia copies of the e-mails and then turn over the computer to you," Chabot said.

Suddenly Raoul erupted, flailing his hands in the air. "Bingo! I told you so. Fucking Antonio might have grabbed Chris, but he had nothing to do with Chris' death. Chris died from strangulation, not being grabbed by the neck."

Getting more and more excited, Raoul tried to get up out of his chair as if he were about to leave. Instead, he made a noise that sounded like a cross between a hiccup and a yelp. Then he grabbed his chest with his right hand and pitched face first onto the tile floor, his head bouncing on the hard surface.

Instantly Chabot jumped out of his chair and moved away, as though Raoul's heart attack was contagious.

"Call nine-one-one, fast!" Fernando said to Manny and ran across the room. He fell to his knees and turned over Raoul, whose face was pale and bloated. Immediately Fernando ripped open Raoul's shirt and began chest compressions, alternating every thirty compressions with mouth to mouth breathing.

Chabot quietly snuck out of the office.

Manny put down the desk phone. "The ambulance is on the way. I'll meet them out front," he said, accidentally knocking over his chair and then running out of the office and down the long hall to the front door.

While Fernando compressed Raoul's chest, he heard a siren coming down Washington Avenue. Moments later he heard a horn blaring and then doors slamming and heavy footsteps in the hallway.

Suddenly two medics burst into the office with Manny close behind.

"Make way," the older of the two medics said to Fernando, who then moved away from Raoul.

The older medic quickly unpacked a defibrillator and placed the paddles on Raoul's naked chest. He hit the power button and immediately Raoul's body jumped and twitched on the tile floor. He went back and forth between manual compressions and the defibrillator.

Meanwhile, the other medic started an IV in Raoul's arm. He turned to Fernando and Manny. "Why don't you guys wait in the sitting area by the front door. We're gonna need to bring a stretcher in here soon."

"Okay," Manny said, motioning for Fernando to follow.

"I don't know, I have a bad feeling about this," Fernando said, tagging along behind. He hated to leave Raoul. Just a feeling he had.

They sat in the narrow corridor at the end of the hallway and waited. A few minutes later the younger medic walked out to the ambulance without speaking to them. He came back with a stretcher.

Moments later the two medics came down the hallway pushing the stretcher. A sheet covered Raoul.

Fernando froze when he saw the sheet over Raoul.

Manny didn't freeze. "Is he going to make it?" Manny asked the medics as they went by.

The older medic shook his head subtly as they pushed the stretcher out the front door.

As the ambulance drove off Manny came over to Fernando, grabbed his shoulder, and gave it a squeeze. "Well...I'm sorry about Raoul, but at least Antonio's not the only suspect. Now we know Chris was blackmailing Ziggy. What better motive for getting rid of Chris?"

Fernando nodded and then watched Manny walk down the hallway to his office. Feeling lost, Fernando sat there for a few minutes before leaving. When he finally left, he turned and walked one block south on Washington Avenue to the Santa Fe Plaza. He found an empty bench near the Bandstand and sat there alone brooding, not knowing what to do or where to go. He wiped a few tears from his eyes.

Fernando couldn't wrap his mind around the fact that Raoul Garcia was dead. It didn't seem possible. Raoul always loomed larger than life, ubiquitous and indomitable. He'd defended everyone from bomb-throwing hippies to tax-evading CEOs and almost always got an acquittal. Raoul was a legal genius, a Santa Fe monument. The only thing he wasn't was immortal.

# 18

Fernando lost all sense of time sitting on the Plaza, remembering a lifetime of Raoul Garcia memories. In many ways the two of them had parallel lives. He joined the Santa Fe Police Department at the same time Raoul finished law school and started his law practice. So many times over the years their paths had crossed, sometimes friendly, sometimes downright contentious. Though Fernando hated to admit it, he and Raoul were very much alike: prickly, at times misanthropic, and often skeptical of everything and everyone.

When his cell phone rang, Fernando expected to hear Antonio's voice since it was close to Noon when the big man usually called. Instead, it was the voice of someone he didn't recognize.

"This is Sammy Logan, Mary Logan's son," the stranger said. "You gave her one of your cards when you stopped by to talk to her."

Now Fernando remembered. The red-headed kid with a bad complexion and a worse temper who'd given him a hard time out on Agua Fria Street. He'd had to teach the kid some manners after the young hothead punched him.

"Yeah, I remember," Fernando said, in a not very friendly tone of voice.

Now the kid burst out weeping.

Embarrassed, Fernando wondered if he'd been too hard on the kid. Should he apologize? He never knew what to do when people started to cry in his presence, especially when it was a reaction to something he did or didn't do. "What"s the matter, son?"

"My mom, she's dead," the kid cried. "I think she overdosed."

"Wait...did you call an ambulance?" Fernando asked, his public servant side kicking in instantly.

"Yah...they're here now...I don't know what to do...she's gone—" the kid trailed off.

Fernando looked around, as if looking for someone else who could help the kid, but there was no one else, only him. So he bit the bullet and said, "Okay, hold on. I'll be there shortly."

After clicking off, Fernando hurried up to Marcy Street and climbed into his Cherokee. Two dead bodies in one day were two more than he'd bargained for, but what could he do? He'd already told the kid he was coming. He drove around the Paseo to South Guadalupe Street and over to Agua Fria Street, where he retraced the route to Mary Logan's house on Antonio Lane. This time, thinking about the name of the lane spooked him. Was Antonio next? After all, the big man hadn't called today. Would Antonio be corpse number three today?

He turned left on Antonio Lane and drove down to the tumbledown L-shaped adobe he'd visited before. He noticed an ambulance parked in the drive, blocking the entrance to the dirt patch in front of the house. Sammy Logan and two men from the ambulance stood talking in the drive. From the looks of it the two men were interviewing Sammy, getting what information they needed.

Fernando saw a stretcher already in the rear of the ambulance, so he parked off to the side so as not to block the ambulance. When Sammy saw him get out of the Cherokee, he came over to meet him. "She's gone," he said, tears sliding down his cheeks.

"Sorry to-" Fernando started to say, but the kid grabbed and hugged him, weeping on his shoulder.

Embarrassed, Fernando didn't know how to respond. He'd never been good in these situations. Another of his many flaws, as Estelle often pointed out. Finally he hugged the kid back, just to get him to let go. "There, there, it'll be okay," he said, patting the kid lightly on his back.

When the kid released him, Fernando moved over to the two men, one of whom he knew from past encounters. Burt Simon or Simmons, he couldn't remember the man's last name.

"Afternoon, Fernando," Burt said. He motioned to the stretcher inside the ambulance. "Looks like the kid's mother overdosed on Fentanyl. We found pills all over her bedroom."

Fernando nodded. "So Sammy said."

"The kid's only seventeen, so we'll contact the police and have them send a social worker out to deal with him," Burt said. "Can you stay with him until the social worker gets here?"

Fernando looked around, wanting to say no. "Okay, I guess I can do that," he said finally. He stood back while Burt and his helper finished their interview with Sammy. When the ambulance drove off, he put his arm around Sammy's shoulders and led him inside the house. They sat on the plaid sofa in the living room. The kid had stopped crying now, which made Fernando feel more comfortable. Providing emotional support in times of tragedy had never been his strong suit, but he had to do something to help the kid. What?

"They're sending a social worker to help you," Fernando said finally. "I'll sit with you until they arrive."

The kid nodded, sad and miserable, looking to Fernando for help. The kid's neediness unsettled Fernando. Ironically, the last time he'd encountered Sammy, the kid had punched him.

"Listen, do you have any family we need to call...people who will help you?" Fernando asked.

The kid nodded. "Yeah, an older sister, Karen. She's an English teacher at Santa Fe High. Her classes should be over by now."

"Good, let's call her, then," Fernando said.

Sammy took out his cell phone and clicked on a telephone number. Then he handed the cell phone to Fernando.

"Oh...okay," Fernando said, surprised. He took the phone from Sammy and waited for the sister to answer.

After a few rings a youthful sounding voice said, "Hi, Sammy, what's up?"

Fernando sighed. "Uh...Karen, this is Fernando Lopez, I'm a former police detective and-"

"Is Sammy okay?" Karen interrupted, a note of hysteria creeping into her voice.

"Yes, I'm sorry," Fernando said. "Sammy's fine, but I'm afraid I have bad news about your mother. An ambulance just took her to Christus Saint Vincent Hospital. They think she had an overdose of fentanyl."

"Oh my God! I knew this was going to happen," Karen said. "She's been taking too much of that stuff. Is Sammy alone there?"

"No, I'm here with him now...and the police are sending a social worker out to help," Fernando said. "I'll stay with Sammy until the social worker arrives. Can you come over to talk with them?"

"Yes, I'm done for the day," Karen said. "I'll be right over."

Fernando handed Sammy his phone. "She's on her way."

They sat in an awkward silence, waiting for Karen to arrive. Finally Sammy broke the silence. "I tried to keep the drug dealer away from her," Sammy said. "I told him I would kill him if something happened to my mother."

"You're talking about this Joey Alhambra guy who works with Doctor Ziggy?" Fernando asked.

Sammy nodded. "I warned him. Now I'll have to kill him, just like I said I would. I have my father's gun. He showed me how to use it...."

That worried Fernando big time. "No, wait...don't do anything foolish. Let the police take care of the drug dealer. They'll find and arrest Alhambra. It's their job...they have the manpower."

"I told him what I would do," Sammy replied. "I plan to keep my word."

Fernando bit his tongue. What could he say to dissuade Sammy? Better to say nothing and hope chance and circumstance would intervene and prevent Sammy from seeking revenge.

Minutes later Fernando heard a car pull into the driveway outside. He went to the front door and saw a woman climb out of her VW Passat and walk quickly over to the door.

"Mister Lopez?" she asked as she approached. She looked to be in her mid-thirties, with short, curly brown hair, and a friendly smile. She wore a gray business suit over a white blouse.

"Yes, Sammy's inside here," Fernando said, opening and holding the door open for her.

Karen stepped inside and ran over to Sammy. They hugged on the sofa for several minutes, Sammy sobbing quietly on her shoulder. Karen patted him on the back, whispering into his ear.

Fernando stayed back, allowing the two siblings time to comfort each other. After a while Karen pulled away from Sammy and turned to Fernando. "What now? What do I have to do?"

"The social worker will be here shortly," Fernando said. "They'll want you to come down to Christus Saint Vincent to take care of the paperwork. And to provide for Sammy."

Karen nodded. She turned to Sammy. "You can come and live with me for the time being. We'll be okay, honey. We'll get through this, I promise."

Sammy shook his head. "Okay, but I want to stay here. This is my home, I'm not going anywhere."

Karen did not respond.

Neither did Fernando. It wasn't his place. Instead he handed Karen a business card and said, "Here's my card. Sammy also has one. Call me if you need help with anything. I'm always available."

Karen glanced at Sammy. "I might take you up on that."

# 19

Feeling ill at ease, Fernando climbed into his Cherokee and drove back to Agua Fria Street, where he turned right and headed for the Paseo. He didn't trust Sammy Logan one bit. The kid had a gun and claimed to know how to use it, even though the kid looked and acted like he didn't know shit about how to handle a weapon. All they needed today was another dead body, Sammy's or whomever the kid tried to shoot. Didn't make any difference.

Fernando castigated himself. He probably should have taken away Sammy's gun, by force if necessary. Yet another thing he regretted not doing. Add it to that load of remorse he carried with him everywhere. The longer he lived, the heavier the load became.

Coming up to South Guadalupe Street he was surprised to see a long line of cars backed up to the Paseo. At first he thought it might be a funeral, but he saw no hearse or police presence. The only time he could remember seeing this much traffic on the Paseo was during the Santa Fe Fiesta in September, over a month away, or the equally popular Indian Market in late August. He decided to check out what was happening, so he pulled into the big parking lot at the Santa Fe Railyard and walked to West Alameda Street headed for the Plaza.

It took him a good fifteen minutes, dodging traffic and honking horns, to walk to the Plaza. He caught a glimpse of the crowd when he cut over to San Francisco Street. Looked like a crowd of about a hundred people were gathered around the bandstand with more entering from the various side streets. Then he saw the banner: 'RIP Raoul Garcia!' Santa Fe had somehow heard of Raoul's death and come to pay their respects. Stunned by what he saw, Fernando paused at the northwest corner of the Plaza, across Palace Avenue from the New Mexico Museum of Art. From here he could watch the spontaneous memorial.

Even though he had his issues with Raoul, who had been a thorn in his side the entire thirty years he'd been a member of the Santa Fe Police Department, Fernando knew that Raoul was probably the most well-known, if not universally loved, person in Santa Fe. Back in the day he'd made his mark defending hippie anarchists and La Raza radicals. In today's woefully bifurcated society, he mostly defended the rapidly growing homeless population and, conversely, the increasingly wealthy imports from the East and West coasts. For years people had begged Raoul to run for City Council or Mayor, but he'd always refused, referring to City Hall as 'Swine Hall,' the very place where one City Council after another had sold out Santa Fe to greedy developers and their filthy lust for gentrification.

On the bandstand now someone was speaking through a bull-horn, praising Raoul for his generosity and the *pro bono* work he'd done for the homeless and Santa Fe's underclass. Most of what he said was lost in the roar of the crowd, who applauded at everything, nonstop. The speaker ended by shouting: "Let's build a statue of Raoul on the Plaza to replace the obelisk that was torn down by criminals and outsiders! Let's name the Plaza after Raoul!" The audience shouted their agreement.

One speaker after another followed, praising Raoul for all he had accomplished fighting the evil forces of gentrification in Santa Fe, which made Fernando smile. What had they accomplished by their never-ending fight against gentrification? Not much of anything.

Then he caught a glimpse of Manny walking down Washington Avenue to the northeastern corner of the Plaza. Fernando walked across the Plaza, through the crowd, to join Manny who stood on the sidewalk shaking his head.

Fernando opened his arms wide. "What the hell?"

"One of the medics called the TV stations, all four of them!" Manny said, disgusted. "Our switchboard has been inundated with calls from the media. Everyone loves Raoul now that he's dead."

Fernando laughed. "More popular dead than alive? I don't know, he was pretty popular alive."

"Not with me," Manny said. "He made my life miserable for years."

"Tell me about it," Fernando replied. "What do you think about what Steve Chabot told us, that Chris was trying to blackmail Ziggy?"

"Just another primary suspect," Manny said. "We'll have to bring Ziggy in again for questioning. I'd still like to talk to Antonio first, but where the hell is he? Nobody can seem to find him."

Fernando held his tongue.

Manny stared at Fernando, waiting for him to come clean with some sort of confession or whatever.

"Have you heard about Mary Logan, another of the three witnesses in the Chabot murder?" Fernando asked, changing the subject.

Manny shook his head. "Why?"

"She apparently overdosed on fentanyl," Fernando said. "Her dealer was Ziggy's man, Joey Alhambra. Now her seventeen-year-old son Sammy is vowing to kill Alhambra."

"How do you know all this?" Manny asked.

"I just came from Mary Logan's home. The son called me this morning to tell me she'd died."

"Great," Manny said. "Just what we need, another kid with a gun trying to shoot someone. Last week on Airport Road we had a fourteen-year-old kid shoot a fifteen-year-old kid over a fucking bicycle."

"Too many guns...and too easy to get," Fernando said.

Manny nodded. Then he glanced at Fernando and asked, "So tell me, when are you ever gonna bring in Antonio for questioning? I'm starting to get impatient. And the Chief is going bonkers."

Fernando laughed. "I don't have Antonio to bring in. I told you, I don't know where the hell he's hiding," he said, which was sort of true. Sort of.

"Well, remind Antonio the longer he waits to come in, the worse it'll look," Manny said. "He should know this."

"I'll tell him," Fernando said, saluting. Then he turned and walked down San Francisco Street, away from the noisy gathering on the Plaza. He took his time walking down to his Cherokee in the Railyard parking lot. And he took his time driving around the Paseo to Acequia Madre Street. Why hurry? He was retired, or at least semi-retired, whatever that meant.

Surprised, Fernando spotted Estelle's Camry when he pulled into their driveway. He parked behind the Camry and walked across their patio to the kitchen door. When he opened the door he was surprised again to see Estelle sitting at the kitchen table drinking a glass of white wine. Estelle only drank wine with dinner.

"What's the occasion?" he asked.

Estelle raised her glass. "Raoul Garcia died today."

"I know. I was there," Fernando replied, walking to the refrigerator and helping himself to a Modelo. Then he joined Estelle at the kitchen table and explained what had happened in Manny's office that afternoon.

Estelle shook her head. "He was a great man. He helped so many poor and homeless people...."

"Yeah, so I keep hearing," Fernando said, not prepared to grant Raoul sainthood, as apparently most Santa Feans were. Saint Raoul?

Estelle gave him the Evil Eye. "You seem dubious?"

Fernando shrugged. "We had our issues, Raoul and I. He was a sonofabitch when we arrested one of his clients."

They argued about Raoul while they finished their drinks. Then Estelle said, "I don't feel like cooking tonight. Why don't we go out to dinner."

Fernando agreed. "Where do you want to go?"

"How about La Choza, we haven't been there in a while?" Estelle said.

"Good choice."

## 20

Fernando moved slowly through the dimly lit room toward the sound of weeping in the next room. The door to the room hung ajar, as though someone had broken down the door earlier. Candlelight cast a dull yellow glow on the wooden floor as he entered the room. Straight ahead he saw a window wide open, its curtains flailing violently in the wind gusts that battered the window. There, under the window, he spotted an ancient woman sitting on a bed, her face partly illuminated by the candlelight and partly in shadow. Weeping softly, she turned her wrinkled face to look at him while cradling a bundle wrapped in blankets. Then she held out the bundle for him to see. When she parted the blankets, he saw the face of a newborn infant, its eyes and mouth frozen open in a grimace of death. And something else. He recognized the face instantly. It was his face on the baby!

"Get away...take it away!" he screamed at the death face. He kicked at the bedclothes that strapped him to the bed, smothering him.

"Fernando, wake up! You're scaring me!" Estelle yelled and jumped out of bed. She came around to his side of the bed and shook him violently.

Fernando's eyes snapped open. He found himself staring into Estelle's angry face. "Jesus, what's wrong with you?" she asked.

Fernando tried to shake it off. "Another nightmare. I can't shake this nightmare. It comes back every night, I don't know what to do."

"Well, do something," Estelle said. "I'm so tired of waking up like this. I'm exhausted."

She checked the nightstand clock and cursed. Then she went into the bathroom to shower and get dressed, even though it was a bit early.

He felt like a fool. He laid low until Estelle had dressed and made her way to the kitchen. When he smelled coffee, he climbed out of bed, slipped on his jeans, and shuffled barefoot to the kitchen.

Estelle poured him a cup of coffee and handed it to him. "Maybe you should go back to the doctor, get some different medication. Not for depression, but something for night terrors or whatever you're having."

"Night terrors?"

"Yes, it's like a nightmare, except you move your arms and legs, sometimes you even get out of bed," Estelle explained.

"Do I get out of bed and move around?" Fernando asked.

Estelle lowered her head. "I suppose not, but you have been known to toss and turn and flail your arms. Everything but."

Fernando sighed. "I don't know what to do. You want me to tell you about my nightmare?"

"God no," she said, leaving the kitchen table. She went back to the bedroom to finish getting ready for work.

He took his coffee outside to the patio and sat on his bench, where he always sat. He was a bit obsessive-compulsive and didn't bother hiding it. Just didn't give a damn. He liked his routines. It was as simple as that.

Later, after Estelle left for work, he was still sitting on the patio trying to figure out his nightmare. It made no sense to him. Why the same nightmare, night after night? What did it mean?

Finally he gave up and went back in the house and finished dressing. He made himself a green chile cheese omelet for breakfast and washed it down with more coffee. He could not get enough coffee these days. Needed the boost. Then he went for a leisurely walk on Acequia Madre Street. His morning walks were the only exercise he bothered with these days. Anything more strenuous bored him.

When he returned he found his cell phone ringing on the kitchen counter. He saw the name and grabbed the phone quickly before it could stop ringing. "Antonio, glad you called—"

"Well, you might not be so glad when I tell you what's happening here," Antonio barked.

"Where are you?" Fernando asked.

"I'm at Rancho Nirvana," Antonio replied. "I've come to settle things with Ziggy and Joey Alhambra, but there's this crazy kid here shooting the place up and taking hostages."

Fernando's spirits sank. He sat down at the kitchen table, fearing the worst. Sammy Logan?

"You listening?" Antonio asked. "He's got this long barrel Colt pistol that he waves around like a fucking baton. He's got Ziggy and a couple of other people inside. I don't know what the hell he's doing."

"I think it must be Sammy Logan, Mary Logan's son," Fernando said. "He's after Joey Alhambra for supplying his mother with fentanyl. She's dead. She overdosed yesterday."

"Jesus...." Antonio said.

"Okay, I'm on my way out there. Wait for me before you do anything."

Antonio muttered something and clicked off.

Pissed at this turn of events, Fernando went into his study and strapped on his holster. He checked to make sure his Smith & Wesson was loaded and then locked the house and walked to his Cherokee.

He followed the usual route, taking the Paseo around to Old Santa Fe Trail and the Old Las Vegas Highway. He had no idea what he would find at Rancho Nirvana or how to go about disarming Sammy Logan. When he spotted the Cañoncito Church he stopped worrying about his lack of a plan. Better to wait until he arrived, check out the situation and then react. From his experience, the most detailed plans fall apart as soon as the shooting started anyway.

Fernando turned right and followed the road down into the canyon. Approaching the Rancho Nirvana driveway he saw no sign of Antonio's Wrangler. Up in the parking lot he did see Sammy Logan's Ford Fiesta parked next to Ziggy's L.L Bean Outback. No sign of the black Escalade he'd seen earlier, which told him Joey Alhambra, the drug dealer, was not on the premises.

He pulled in beside the small Ford Fiesta, noticing its dented fenders and cracked windshield. He climbed out of the Cherokee and started to walk up the flagstone path to the main building.

"Pop!...Pop!...Pop!" suddenly came from the veranda on the front of the building. The bullets kicked up dirt on the left side of the path. Fernando dove to his right, landing in a patch of snake grass and cursing loudly.

"Stop shooting at me, you fucking idiot!" Fernando screamed at Sammy, who tried to hide behind a wooden post on the veranda, as if that post would allow him to conceal his identity. As if!

"I'm here to help you, goddamnit! Put the gun away!" Fernando shouted.

Sammy lowered his gun, a pistol with an extra long barrel, just as Antonio had said. The kid came out from behind the post tentatively. He waited while Fernando climbed the path.

Not sure of Sammy's intentions, Fernando moved carefully up the hill, ready to hit the dirt if Sammy made any quick moves. He had his hand on his Smith & Wesson, just in case. He had no idea what he would do with it if Sammy started shooting. The last thing he wanted to do was shoot the kid. He had enough dead bodies on his conscience, he didn't need any more, especially not a fucking teenager.

"What do you want?" Sammy asked.

"To stop you from doing something you'll regret, what do you think?" Fernando shot back. "You're young, you don't want to spend the next ten to twenty years in prison."

"I don't care, I'm gonna shoot Joey for killing my mom," the kid replied, lowering his head. "Thing is, he's not here, so I'll have to come back."

"Give me the gun, Sammy," Fernando said, holding out his hand.

Sammy raised his pistol and pointed it at Fernando's gut.

Fernando shook his head. "All right, don't give me the gun, fuck off! Where is everybody, anyway?"

Sammy pointed to the front door.

Fernando opened the door and walked inside to the big room with the now familiar rows of old church pews facing the podium and white board. Ziggy's church of peyote or whatever he called it.

Ziggy himself sat on the floor behind the podium, leaning back against the wall. The only other person in the room was a young woman with short-cropped blond hair, nose and eye-brow rings, and strings of love heads hanging between her breasts, all but exposed under her skimpy halter top. The woman lay on a pew in the last aisle, eyes closed. Maybe dead, Fernando couldn't tell.

"Miss, are you okay?" Fernando said, peering down at her.

"I'm meditating, don't disturb me," she replied.

So Fernando walked over to where Ziggy sat on the floor, eyes wide open as if he'd just seen a ghost or something equally shocking. Sammy Logan?

Then Fernando noticed the swelling and the blood on the right side of Ziggy's face. Looked like the kid had pistol-whipped him.

"What happened?" Fernando asked.

"The little shit hit me with his fucking gun, what do you think?" Ziggy responded. "He wants to kill Joey."

"Where is Alhambra?" Fernando asked.

"He's making his rounds up north," Ziggy said. "Should be back sometime tomorrow."

"Well, you might want to warn him about Sammy."

"Hah! It's Doctor Ziggy's considered opinion that young Mister Logan couldn't hit a barn if he were standing inside," Ziggy said. "It's the kid who should be worried about Joey. Joey will kill him."

Fernando couldn't argue with that. So he said nothing.

For a moment he was tempted to ask Ziggy about being blackmailed by Chris Chabot but decided against it. It wasn't Fernando's play to make. Let Manny tighten the noose.

Leaving, Fernando opened the door and stepped outside. He saw Sammy walking down the path to the parking lot, where he climbed into his Ford Fiesta and squealed off in the dirt lot, leaving a cloud of dust behind.

Fernando watched the Fiesta career down the dirt road and then turn onto the paved road leading out of Apache Canyon. He supposed Sammy would be back tomorrow looking to shoot Alhambra. If Alhambra showed up, the situation could get dicey. Which meant he too would have to return in order to keep the peace or whatever he was doing here. He'd lost track.

First, however, he needed to talk to Antonio, who he was supposed to be helping. Funny thing, though, Antonio didn't seem to need much help. So what was he doing here?

# 21

Before doing anything else Fernando called Antonio on his cell phone, thinking the big man had turned on his phone now that he'd returned to the Santa Fe area. No such luck. Whether he liked it or not, he would still have to wait until Antonio called him. Which pissed him off. If Antonio wanted his help, then he should at least make himself available.

Irritated by just about everything that he'd done today, he drove back into Santa Fe on the Old Las Vegas Highway. When he turned onto the Paseo he continued on by Acequia Madre and instead turned right on Canyon Road. He drove up to the parking lot between his old office and Ruby's gallery, Three Cities of Spain. Ruby still hadn't rented his old office. She still harbored the hope that he might change his mind and reopen his office. He was tempted, but if he did Estelle would go ballistic.

He parked beside Ruby's Honda and walked into her gallery. A bell announced his presence as the door closed behind him. "Ruby?" he asked, not seeing her at the front counter.

"Back here," Ruby said from the tiny space she called her lunchroom. "I'm making a turkey sandwich, you want half of it?"

"Sure, I could eat," Fernando said, walking into the lunch room, which consisted of a small counter, a mini refrigerator, a microwave oven, and a Keurig coffee maker. Ruby had a turkey sandwich stuffed with tomato, lettuce, and cheese. She cut the sandwich in half on a wooden cutting board and passed him half on a paper plate. Then she made him a cup of coffee in the Keurig.

"Thanks," Fernando said, noticing Ruby looked a bit subdued today, not her usual ebullient self. "What's up? Trouble with your sister Tessa again?"

"No, after I heard the news, I just can't stop thinking about Raoul," Ruby said. "I can't believe he's gone, you know? Santa Fe without Raoul just doesn't seem possible. I mean, he WAS Santa Fe. He embodied its history, both the good and the bad. It just doesn't seem possible that someone with a presence that large could just disappear like that."

"I know, I feel the same way," Fernando said, dumping sugar and cream into his black coffee.

"We're gonna have to put together a memorial, maybe at El Farol like we did for Wayne Fontenot," Ruby said. "Raoul doesn't have any family. His younger brother Paul died a few years back. As far as I know Rosalie, his legal secretary, is in charge of his affairs."

"You mean the executor of his will?" Fernando asked.

Ruby nodded. "I think so. She told me once that Raoul was leaving everything to the nonprofits he supported. New Mexico Legal Aid, the New Mexico Center on Law and Poverty, the American Civil Liberties Union, and some local Hispanic groups. That sort of thing."

"Sure, we can arrange something at El Farol," Fernando said. "Why not? All of us knew and loved him, more or less. El Farol would be perfect. He was one of the regulars, like the rest of us."

"I'll ask Rosalie to put together a list of people we should invite."

Fernando laughed. "Tell her to make sure the list includes people who not only knew but actually liked Raoul. Remember, Raoul had a lot of enemies."

Ruby smiled. "Kinda pisses me off that the big gorilla didn't take better care of himself," she said.

"He wouldn't have been Raoul if he had," Fernando said. "He was larger than life. And he lived life large."

Ruby was silent for a moment. "It was a heart attack, right?"

"Yeah, I was with him," Fernando said. "We were at a meeting in Manny's office with Steve Chabot. He just collapsed on the floor. I tried to revive him with chest compressions until the medics got there, but it was no use, he was already gone when they arrived."

"What was this meeting about?"

Fernando told her that Steve Chabot had found email on his son's computer revealing that Chris had been trying to blackmail Ziggy.

"So Antonio's off the hook, then," Ruby said.

Fernando shook his head. "No, it just means there are other suspects, namely Ziggy and Joey Alhambra, the drug dealer who's been living at Rancho Nirvana and supplying the peyote."

"Never heard of Joey Alhambra, but I wouldn't put anything past Ziggy," Ruby said. "He's been a druggie for over fifty years, high on LSD back in the day and then mescaline and mushrooms and peyote and anything else he could get his hands on. Like I told you, he used to drive that old psychedelic school bus around Santa Fe with all the young women he could get his hands on, half of them jail bait. He got the idea when Ken Kesey showed up in Santa Fe with his Band of Merry Pranksters driving their old school bus painted psychedelic colors. As I recall Kesey named that bus 'Furthur.' They were quite a sight in stuffy old Santa Fe. That would have been around nineteen sixty-nine or seventy. Do you remember the Pranksters?"

"No, but I remember my parents talking about the crazy hippies in town," Fernando replied. "They always told me to stay away from them."

Ruby laughed. "Well, my mom was a single mother. After she ditched my father, she realized she had a good dose of hippie in her. Those were her wild years. So she took me and Tessa up to Aspen Meadow where Kesey was staying. You might have seen that famous photograph of Kesey's bus parked in Aspen Meadow taken by the great Lisa Law? We were all there. I must have been about ten years old, Tessa maybe five. They made a big impression on my mother. I think that's why she never remarried. Why marry one man when you could remain unattached and party with whoever you wanted, whenever you wanted."

"You think Kesey was a model for Ziggy?" Fernando asked.

"Yeah, Ziggy, or Frank as he was known then, came up to see Kesey too," Ruby said. "He was older, must have been fifteen or sixteen because we saw him riding around in his version of 'Furtur' not long after Kesey left town."

Fernando smiled. "The age of love-ins."

Ruby laughed again. "Believe me, there was a lot of lovin' in Ziggy's bus! That was his thing back then, sex with young girls and psychedelic drugs. I don't know how he ever managed to go legit with these therapy sessions, if he is legit. I still have my doubts."

"He claims to have received an online degree from some university in the Midwest, although he's never very specific about which online university in the Midwest," Fernando said.

"I can imagine."

"And he claims he got his expertise in Peyote from his years in the Native American Church," Fernando added.

"Sure, because belonging to the Native American Church makes his peyote use legal," Ruby said. "Peyote's protected as long as it's used in a religious ceremony, a sacrament."

Ruby finished her sandwich and made herself another cup of coffee. She turned to Fernando. "You want another cup? I can't get through the day without multiple cups of coffee."

Fernando checked his watch. "Well, it's too early for Happy Hour at La Fonda, so why not?"

# 22

Fernando awoke with a raging headache. It wasn't exactly a hangover, but it wasn't exactly not a hangover either. More likely it was from haggling with Ruby all yesterday afternoon about a memorial for Raoul Garcia at El Farol. They'd spent most of the afternoon arguing about who to invite. Then Ruby made the mistake of calling Rosalie Trujillo, Raoul's legal secretary, who informed Ruby in no uncertain terms that Raoul's memorial would not be held in some damned bar but in the magnificent Saint Francis Auditorium of the New Mexico Museum of Art, a fitting venue for such a distinguished person.

"Distinguished? Raoul? You're kidding," Ruby shot back, after which Rosalie slammed down her phone and ended the conversation, forcing Ruby to call back and apologize.

After all was said and done the two of them agreed on a settlement. Rosalie would hold an official memorial for Raoul in Saint Francis Auditorium, while Ruby and Fernando would hold an unofficial memorial at El Farol for the Canyon Road artist crowd and other similar undesirables. Worked for Rosalie, and it worked for Ruby and Fernando.

To celebrate they'd gone over to El Farol for Happy Hour, where they'd hooked up with Blaine Rogers and Ruby's sister Tessa Montez, both heavy drinkers. What followed could have been avoided. Ruby and Blaine got into their usual argument over Jimmy Mackey's paintings, about who had the right to sell them, his ex-wife Ruby or his ex-agent Blaine. The end result was that everyone drank too much and yelled too loudly, including Fernando, until the whole lot of them were asked to leave the premises by the head bartender.

On these mornings when he may or may not be suffering from a hangover, there was only one sure antidote: huevos rancheros and lots of coffee. So Fernando pulled on his jeans and shuffled barefoot down the hall to the kitchen and set to work. After brewing himself a cup of coffee in the Keurig, he gathered his ingredients—eggs, sausage, beans, tortillas and green chile—and worked furiously for a good half hour. The result was a hot plate of huevos rancheros smothered in green chile, which he wolfed down standing at the kitchen counter. After three cups of coffee, he began to feel like he could face the day, whatever it would bring. He took a fourth cup of coffee outside to the patio and relaxed, trying to get rid of his headache. When that didn't work, he went back inside and gobbled two Tylenol and finished dressing.

Somewhere down the hallway he heard his cell phone ringing. Where was his cell phone? He couldn't remember where he'd left it last night. He searched the living room and his study but didn't find it. Then he went back into the kitchen and found the damn thing pushed back into a corner of the counter beside the microwave, where he or Estelle must have put it for safekeeping.

The ringing had stopped by the time Fernando picked up the phone. Seeing Antonio's name on the screen, he hit the redial button and waited. "Antonio!" he said when Antonio answered.

"I'm back," Antonio said.

"Back where? What do you mean?" Fernando asked, puzzled.

"I'm back in Apache Canyon," Antonio said. "I drove in this morning and found a dirt road leading up to a ridge on the other side of the canyon. I can see Rancho Nirvana clearly from here using my binoculars. Alhambra's here now. He came back a little while ago in that black Escalade. I'm planning to go down this afternoon and settle. You wanna join the fun?"

"Yes...I mean, no! What the hell do you plan to do once you get down there?" Fernando asked.

"Whatever I have to do to take care of business," Antonio said.

"You're no longer a cop, remember?" Fernando shot back. "You can't just go in there and expect them to get on their knees and confess."

Antonio laughed. "You're funny. But don't you worry, I have ways of taking care of people like Ziggy and Alhambra. Sounds like a comedy act, doesn't it? Ziggy and Joey."

"I don't know, Antonio, these people could be dangerous, especially Alhambra," Fernando replied. "So wait until I get there, okay? That's the least you can do. The two of us will go in together."

"Like Butch and Sundance," Antonio said.

"Great. They were massacred, if you remember."

"I never stayed for the end of the movie, because I knew what was coming," Antonio responded. "But okay, I'll wait until I see your Cherokee pull into Ziggy's parking lot and then I'll come down and join you. We'll kick some ass. Be like old times."

With that, the connection went dead. Antonio had clicked off.

Fernando could hardly believe what he'd just agreed to. What had he been thinking? That was the problem, he hadn't been thinking clearly. He cursed himself for last night's excesses because it was his own damn fault. Still groggy, his mind wasn't as sharp as he needed it to be.

He wracked his brains for back-up, law enforcement people who had retired or experienced private investigators. The only retiree he could think of was Hank Dixon who for years had been the best sharpshooter on the Santa Fe Police Department's SWAT team, but he was too damned old now. And he couldn't very well ask Manny, now the lead detective at the SFPD, because what he and Antonio were about to do was almost certainly not legal.

Not knowing what to expect at Apache Canyon, Fernando buckled on his holster and out of habit made sure his Smith & Wesson was loaded. It was, so he locked up the house and climbed into his Cherokee. He drove quickly around the Paseo to Old Santa Fe Trail and the Old Las Vegas Highway. He ignored the speed limit, racing by Bobcat Bite. When he saw the Cañoncito Church he slowed down for the turn-off into Apache Canyon. He followed the road around to the driveway into Rancho Nirvana. Ahead he saw both Ziggy's L.L. Bean Outback and Alhambra's black Escalade in the parking lot, just as Antonio had said. Parking at the far end of the parking lot, away from the other vehicles, he jumped out of the Cherokee and stood in the center of the dusty lot waiting for Antonio.

A few minutes later Fernando heard Antonio's Wrangler come bouncing down the main road from the other side of Apache Canyon. Antonio turned into the Rancho Nirvana driveway and pulled into the parking lot. He parked vertically behind both the Outback and the Escalade, so as to prevent Ziggy and Alhambra from fleeing. When Antonio stepped out of the Wrangler, Fernando noticed he wasn't wearing his gun. Not such a good idea, given the presence of Alhambra.

Fernando joined Antonio. "You're not armed?"

"I don't need a gun to deal with these clowns," Antonio replied, starting up the flagstone trail to the main building.

Fernando took out his iphone. He opened the Voice Memos app and clicked on record. Then he put the iphone back in his shirt pocket and followed Antonio, trying to keep up. Ahead he saw Ziggy gathering an armful of firewood from a lean-to built on the side of the main building. Ziggy turned to carry the firewood to the fire circle behind him when he spotted Antonio and Fernando coming fast up the flagstone path. He froze, dropping the load of wood at his feet. Then he bent over and picked up one piece of wood, which he tucked under his arm.

"Antonio! Where you been, man? Everyone's looking for you," Ziggy said, wearing a weird paisley shirt and even weirder cotton bloomers, bell-bottoms. Looked like he was wearing his pajamas.

"I been worried about you, bro," Ziggy continued, trying his best to sound conciliatory, if not downright friendly. Probably because Antonio looked like he was about ready to kill someone, namely Ziggy.

"Bullshit!" Antonio boomed. "You set me up, you motherfucker!"

Fernando stepped forward. "It was you who killed Chris Chabot... because he was blackmailing you," he added.

Ziggy did not respond at first. He shook his head sadly and then glanced at the back porch of the house, as if looking for help from Alhambra. Then he slowly turned to face them.

Without warning, Ziggy swung the piece of wood at Antonio.

Antonio's left hand shot up and caught the piece of wood in his hand. He jerked the wood out of Ziggy's hand and brought it down hard on the right side of Ziggy's face, knocking the skinny old man flat on the ground.

"Owww!" Ziggy yelled. "What's wrong with you, man? After all I've done for you?"

"The only thing you did for me was set me up," Antonio growled, raising the piece of wood.

Fernando tried to intervene, seeing blood oozing from Ziggy's face. "Take it easy, Antonio. He's an old man."

"Old?" Ziggy sputtered. "I'm no older than you are, Lopez."

"Well, in that case, hit him again," Fernando said, taunting Ziggy.

"Enough! Stop right there!" came a loud booming voice from around the corner of the house.

Suddenly a muscular man wearing a black hoodie pulled down low over his jeans and holding a Glock 9 mm. pistol stepped around the corner.

Joey Alhambra.

## 23

"Drop the wood," Alhambra ordered, pointing the Glock at Antonio. Instead of dropping it, Antonio flipped the wood up in the air. It landed at Alhambra's feet.

"Now you," Alhambra said, turning quickly to Fernando. "Throw down your gun...now!"

Fernando took his Smith & Wesson out of its holster and placed it carefully on the ground. He smiled. "So it was you. You killed Chris Chabot. You strangled him with a wire garrote and then carried him out to the fire circle. He was already dead when the ceremony began."

"Yeah, so what?" Alhambra shot back. "He was a poor excuse for a man, always whining about his life. He couldn't get a job, he couldn't get along with his father, he didn't have any money, on and on, one thing after another. Always whining about something. I did him a favor by putting him out of his misery. Now we don't have to listen to his complaints."

"Chris was a lost soul, I'm afraid," Ziggy added sorrowfully. He sat slumped over on the ground holding the right side of his face, blood slowly dripping onto his paisley shirt.

Everyone ignored Ziggy.

"So you killed him," Fernando continued, speaking to Alhambra. "Just like your drugs killed Marry Logan and probably Tom Lujan."

"What drugs?" Alhambra asked.

"Fentanyl and the other shit you peddle here and from your drugmobile," Antonio added.

Alhambra laughed. "Drugmobile? That's a new one. But again, so what? I give them what they need to feel better. To feel happy, or to feel less anxious. I'm their fucking salvation."

Fernando shook his head. "No, you're their executioner."

Just then they heard a car turning into the driveway below. An old brown Ford Fiesta rattled up the driveway to the parking lot and sputtered to a stop, belching smoke and exhaust.

Fernando smiled, in spite of himself. Just what they needed to make the party complete. Sammy Logan.

Alhambra paid no attention to the new arrival, not recognizing the Fiesta.

Suddenly Sammy jumped out of the Fiesta and charged up the flagstone path. "Where is he? I'll kill the fucker!" he shouted, waving his long barrel pistol. He fired off two rounds in the air to make his point.

"Who's that?" Alhambra asked, turning away and moving over to the top of the flagstone path.

Antonio seized the opportunity. The big man lunged at Alhambra, tackling him from behind. Knocked off balance, Alhambra stumbled and then fell forward. He slid a few yards down the hill before managing to scramble to his feet, still holding his Glock.

When Sammy saw his prey, he opened fire. Alhambra returned fire. Both shooters dodged and jumped from one side of the path to the other, shooting randomly at each other. Finally Sammy screamed and fell off the path into a stand of chamisa bushes and lay still.

Meanwhile, Fernando picked up his Smith & Wesson and started down the flagstone path, leaving Antonio watching over Ziggy. Fernando worried about leaving Ziggy with Antonio. He could only hope that Antonio didn't strangle Ziggy with his own two hands.

Halfway down the path he spotted Alhambra climbing into his Escalade. Alhambra had decided to run. He revved up the engine and threw the Escalade in reverse, smashing into the Wrangler parked directly behind it. That gave Alhambra enough room to go forward and make a U turn in the parking lot, spewing dirt and gravel behind it as it slid around in a circle, out from behind the Wrangler.

As the Escalade squealed off in a cloud of dust, Fernando opened fire, trying to hit the rear tires of the Escalade. But the black drugmobile was moving too fast. It turned onto the road in and out of Apache Canyon and quickly disappeared around a curve. Gone.

Now Fernando turned his attention to Sammy, who was struggling to get out of the chamisa bushes while holding his right leg. "Fucker shot me in the leg," Sammy said, limping out of the bushes.

Fernando saw immediately that Sammy's right leg was bleeding profusely. Looked like the bullet might have hit the main artery. The bottom of his right pant leg was soaked in blood.

"Lay down and elevate your leg. Now!" Fernando ordered.

Fernando pushed the kid down and ordered him to lay flat. Taking out his pocket knife, he sliced the kid's blood-soaked jeans from the cuff to above the knee in order to expose the wound, a nasty rip through the calf muscle and maybe the artery. He could tell because of all the blood.

Hurrying now, Fernando took the bandana he carried in his rear pocket and used it as a tourniquet, pulling the knot tight and tighter until the kid yelped. "We have to get you to an emergency room fast."

By this time Antonio and Ziggy had joined them. "Jesus, that's a lot of blood," Antonio said.

"Yeah, we need to get him to the emergency room as fast as possible," Fernando said and then pointed to Ziggy. "You...take Sammy to the ER at Christus Saint Vincent Hospital."

"Me? Why should I do it?" Ziggy complained.

"Because this is all your fault," Fernando replied. "Everything that's happened here."

Antonio remained deadly silent. He walked over to Ziggy and grabbed him by the neck with one of his huge hands. Then he picked up the little man with the funny handlebar mustache by the neck and let him dangle. "You take him to the ER now or I will let you suffocate."

Ziggy kicked his feet and gurgled, trying to speak. He nodded yes to make Antonio understand.

Antonio dropped the little man on the ground. Ziggy landed on his ass with a big plopping sound. "Owww, you hurt my jaw," Ziggy said, massaging the bruised side of his face.

"That's not all that's going to hurt unless you get your ass moving," Antonio said. "Let's go." With that Antonio picked up Sammy and carried him down the path to Ziggy's L.L. Bean Outback.

Ziggy followed Antonio, grumbling. Not a happy camper, he folded down the backseats of the Outback to make a flat bed for the kid, and then Antonio laid Sammy down on the carpeted platform.

Fernando grabbed a duffle bag on the floor behind the driver's seat and used it to elevate Sammy's right leg.

"Wait...what'll I do about insurance?" Ziggy asked.

"They have an indigent fund," Fernando said. "Just tell them you found him along the highway in Apache Canyon. Hunting accident. Make up something. You're good at making things up, right? That's your game."

Ziggy, cursing, climbed into the Outback, backed up, and took off fast down the driveway with Sammy bouncing and yelling to slow the fuck down in the rear of the Subaru.

Fernando and Antonio watched the Outback disappear up the road to the highway. As soon as it was out of sight, Fernando turned to Antonio and said, "Let's take this opportunity to check out the bunkhouse where Alhambra is staying. He won't be back for a while and neither will Ziggy."

"Good idea," Antonio said.

"If we can find the drugs he peddles, maybe we can get rid of them," Fernando said. "Save some lives."

They walked back up the flagstone path to the main building. To get to the bunkhouse they followed a side path that ran perpendicular to the main path to a series of outbuildings, including the bunkhouse and what appeared to be an old barn with a caved in roof. The bunkhouse had slat siding, gray and rotting, and a pitched roof with what looked like primitive cedar shingles. The single window in front looked black with layers of dirt and mold.

"Jesus," Antonio said, opening the flimsy wooden door and looking inside. "He actually lives here?"

Fernando followed Antonio into the bunkhouse, which hadn't ben finished or insulated inside. Without the usual drywall, these walls consisted of two-by-fours and the outside slats, nothing else. A rusted black wood stove stood in the very center of the one-room building, buttressed by two wooden chairs. Off to the left was a picnic table and a nearby counter built out of two-by-fours and particle board. On the counter they saw a Coleman camping stove, a stack of paper plates and plastic utensils, and a large Igloo cooler.

Antonio pointed to the Coleman lanterns scattered around the room. "No electricity or running water."

On the right side of the room stood three double bunk beds, sleeping up to six people. Only one of the bunks had a pillow and sleeping bag on top, where Alhambra had been sleeping. Between the wood stove and the bunk beds was a rear door that opened up on another short flagstone path to a small gray outhouse that tilted noticeably to the left, as if ready to implode.

Fernando didn't see any cabinets or closets where Alhambra could hide his drugs, so he walked around the perimeter of the room searching for secret hiding places. The first time he saw nothing suspicious. The second time he noticed an area rug along the wall behind the picnic table. The placement made no sense. No one would walk there intentionally.

"The rug? I know," Antonio said. "I was about to say something."

Fernando bent down and pulled up the rug, revealing a sheet of particle board. Underneath the particle board he found a heavy wooden box with a lid buried in the floor. When he opened the lid, he found two cherry red carry-on suitcases zipped and locked tight.

"Here, let me get them," Antonio said, reaching in and grabbing one suitcase and then the other. He placed them on the picnic table side by side.

Fernando took out his lock pick and went to work. When he opened the first suitcase, they found eight 12x15 inch plastic bags stuffed to the brim with blue pills. Fentanyl.

The second suitcase, when opened, contained four 12x15 inch plastic bags filled with blue pills and four filled with white pills.

"Probably meth," Antonio said, holding up one of the bags of white pills. "There's still a few meth heads around from the last drug epidemic."

"What shall we do with them?" Fernando asked, smiling.

Antonio looked around the room and then pointed to the rear door. "The outhouse. We don't even have to flush."

Fernando laughed. "Have at it. I'll hand the bags to you."

Antonio carried the suitcases out back to the outhouse, which stank to high heaven. Fernando stayed outside, handing the bags one at a time to Antonio, who ripped them open and poured their contents into one of the three holes, varying the hole with each bag. After the last bag had been emptied, he wadded up the plastic bags and tossed them in the center hole.

Antonio stepped out of the outhouse and closed the door, leaving the outhouse exactly as they had found it. "He'll assume we took the drugs...never guess we tossed them in the shitter."

Fernando smiled, imagining Alhambra finding his drugs gone. "And if he does guess correctly and looks into the holes with a flashlight, let him jump in to retrieve them pill by shit-covered pill."

"Now that I would like to see," Antonio said.

## 24

Fernando watched Antonio drive off. He assumed Antonio would return to where he had been hiding in the foothills behind his cabin in the Pecos. He waited until the Wrangler disappeared on the road out of Apache Canyon. Then he pulled out his cell phone and stopped the recording. He rewound the recording to the place he wanted. When he found it he listened to himself say:

*"So it was you. You killed Chris Chabot. You strangled him with a wire garrote and then carried him out to the fire circle. He was already dead when the ceremony began."*

And then he listened to Alhambra's response:

*"Yeah, so what? He was a poor excuse for a man, always whining about his life. He couldn't get a job, he couldn't get along with his father, he didn't have any money, on and on, one thing after another. Always whining about something. I did him a favor by putting him out of his misery. Now we don't have to listen to his complaints."*

Bingo!

He would stop by the Washington Avenue Station when he got back to Santa Fe and let Manny listen. The recording should be enough to change the trajectory of Manny's investigation and put the spotlight on Joey Alhambra, not Antonio. First, though, he wanted to stop by Christus Saint Vincent Hospital and check on Sammy Logan to make sure the kid was okay.

Somehow Fernando felt responsible for Sammy's injury. He kept thinking he should have taken the kid's gun away when Sammy first mentioned it back at the house in Agua Fria. If he had, the kid wouldn't be on his way to the emergency room. One more thing he regretted.

Now that he had a plan, Fernando climbed into his Cherokee and drove out of Apache Canyon. On the Old Las Vegas Highway he drove fast back to Santa Fe, cutting over to Saint Michael's Drive right before the Old Santa Fe Trail exit. Christus Saint Vincent Hospital came into view immediately off to the right. He turned into the parking lot and pulled up in front of the emergency room entrance.

The ER looked positively deserted today, a rarity. Fernando saw only one elderly couple and a teenager with an apparent soccer injury, his left knee wrapped in ice packs. The teen's father kept looking at his watch, irritated at the wait. The elderly couple sat in silence, heads bowed stoically after a lifetime of waiting.

A plump young woman greeted him at the counter. "Can I help you?" she asked suspiciously, as though she'd taken one look at him and expected trouble. Her look said: Here comes trouble!

Ignoring her attitude, Fernando said, "I'm here to check on a teenager who was brought in earlier this afternoon with a gunshot wound to his leg. His name's Sammy Logan."

The young woman gave him the Evil Eye. "Are you family?"

"No, just a friend wanting to check on him," Fernando replied.

She turned to her computer and clicked a few keys. "He's in emergency surgery now. You can wait for him in his room, two twenty-seven, or in the waiting room next to the surgical ICU."

Fernando nodded. "Where's that waiting room?"

She pointed down the hallway, already bored with the conversation.

"Thanks, you've been a big help," Fernando said sarcastically.

He walked to the end of the hallway, where he found a sign directing him to the surgical ICU around the corner. He found four other people waiting there, with an attendant sitting at a desk.

"Who are you waiting for?" the attendant asked.

"Sammy Logan," Fernando said, taking a seat in the rear of the room, where he waited impatiently. And waited.

Over an hour later Fernando was bored out of his mind, so he pulled out his cell phone and emailed Manny, informing him that he had a recording of Joey Alhambra admitting to killing Chris Chabot and that he would bring the recording in to his office late this afternoon. After he sent the email, he wondered if he should have included the recording on the email he sent Manny. Problem was, he didn't know how to send a phone recording by email. To find out, he googled 'how to send an iphone recording' and found several suggestions. He tried the first two, becoming increasingly frustrated by his attempts to attach a Voice Memo file to an email until he finally said the hell with it. He had limited patience for technology. Another of his many shortcomings, he realized.

Finally a nurse wearing a white uniform entered the waiting room and spoke with the attendant. He came over to Fernando and said, "You can see Mister Logan now, if you wish. He's awake."

Fernando thanked the attendant and walked into the ICU. Sammy was lying on a gurney with his right leg raised.

One of the doctors wearing a surgical cap and gown came over to greet Fernando as he approached Sammy's bed. The doctor introduced himself and said Sammy had tolerated the surgery well.

"The bullet punctured the main artery in the leg and shredded part of the muscle," the doctor said. "We patched it up, but he'll need support when he leaves the hospital. We'll keep him overnight, just to make sure everything's healing as it should, and then send him home tomorrow morning if all goes well. Like I said, he'll need support for a while and probably physical therapy to loosen the leg muscle that's been badly damaged."

"Okay, I'll call his older sister. I think he can stay with her while he recovers," Fernando said.

Sammy's eyes were closed when Fernando moved over to his bedside. "Sammy, can you hear me?" he asked.

Sammy stirred, opening his eyes slightly.

"Doc said your surgery went well—he said you could probably go home tomorrow morning," Fernando said. "I'll call your sister and tell her the news."

Sammy tried to speak. "Did...you...kill...him," he whispered, his voice very weak and cracking.

"No...." Fernando replied and left it at that. A longer explanation could come later. Much later.

Sammy closed his eyes again and appeared to sleep.

Fernando thanked the doctor and went back into the waiting room to call Sammy's sister, Karen. He'd written down her number in his pocket notebook when he'd talked to her in Agua Fria.

Karen answered right away. "You're lucky this is Saturday, otherwise I wouldn't be home," she said.

Fernando had no idea it was Saturday. Since retiring he had not done a very good job of keeping track of the days of the week, since they all seemed the same. Laughing, he said, "I guess so. I'm calling to let you know that Sammy's in Christus Saint Vincent Hospital."

"I know, they called me earlier as the next of kin," Karen said.

"Good. So you know about the leg wound," Fernando said. "He's out of surgery and seems to be sleeping now. The doc said he could probably come home tomorrow morning, but that he'll need physical therapy because the leg muscle was damaged by the bullet."

"Okay, he can stay with me until he gets back on his feet. No pun intended," she said, laughing. "I'll be over to check on him this evening. Do you know what room he'll be in?"

"Two twenty-seven, I was told."

"Thanks, Mister Lopez," she said. "I appreciate your help. Sammy's a handful, as I'm sure you've noticed."

"That I have," Fernando said.

## 25

Fernando backed away from the infant's death face, his death face. The old woman sitting on the bed held out the bundle for him to take, an offering. Smiling, her wrinkles tightened in her face. She laughed at him as he stumbled backwards, trying to get away. He turned and ran out of the dark room splashed with candlelight. He collided with a heavy dresser near the door, knocking over the candle on top. He smelled smoke. Something was burning on the floor.

Suddenly the room burst into flames behind him. The flames licked his clothing and scorched his face. He staggered into the hallway and ran for the front door of the house, but as he ran the hallway seemed to shrink around him, making him crouch and hold out his hands to try to hold back the walls as they squeezed in on him, tighter and tighter. He fell to his knees, the ceiling squeezing down on him until he couldn't move, only scream.

"Heeeeelp!" he screamed in bed. His arms and legs thrashed against the blankets as he tried to run for his life.

Suddenly he heard bells ringing somewhere off in the distance. Were they tolling for him?

He began to wake up as Estelle burst into the bedroom. "Why are you screaming? What's the matter with you now?"

Cracking open his eyes, he saw that Estelle was dressed for church. That explained the church bells. It was Sunday. Estelle went to mass almost every Sunday morning. He didn't. He'd lost his faith years ago.

"Why are you having these nightmares?" Estelle continued.

"I don't know," was all Fernando could think to say.

"Well...I saved you half of my omelet and some coffee," Estelle said, her tone softening. "Come have breakfast."

Feeling foolish, Fernando crawled out of bed and slipped into his jeans and shuffled barefoot down the hall to their kitchen.

Estelle had set a place at the table for him, with the omelet already on a plate and a cup of steaming coffee waiting for him. At first he ignored the omelet but took a long drink of coffee. The jolt of caffeine helped clear his mind, so he took another. And another.

"I mean, why have you started having these nightmares?" Estelle asked. "Why now?"

Fernando shook his head. "I don't know, but it's the same dream every night. The same nightmare."

"Do you remember it? Tell me about it."

"I do...but it'll sound crazy," Fernando said, by way of apology. "I'm in this dark old house trying to find my way out. While I'm searching for an exit I hear someone weeping from a room deep in the house. I can't see in the dark, but I move slowly toward the weeping sound. Finally I enter a room lit by candlelight where an old woman sits on a bed holding a dead baby in her arms. She offers me the baby, but when she does I see the baby has my face. It's me...as a baby...dead."

Estelle stared at him without commenting.

"Then I bolt, I find myself running down a long hallway that keeps shrinking," Fernando continues. "The walls and ceiling are closing in on me, pinning me. I can't move!"

Now Estelle spoke. "Well, it doesn't take a shrink to know what that nightmare means. "Birth, death, it's about mortality: your mortality. When you encounter death, you try to escape, running down that hallway, but the walls shrink around you. Like space, time is running out for you. Your subconscious is recognizing and trying to come to terms with your mortality, don't you see?"

Fernando nodded, impressed by Estelle's interpretation. He didn't know what to say in response. He would have to give this some thought. Estelle had amazing powers of deduction. Or maybe induction. Whatever it was that allowed her to decipher his subconscious eruptions.

Estelle left the kitchen and then came back momentarily with her purse. "Anyway, I'm on my way to mass. I'll be home for lunch."

Fernando nodded again as she walked out the kitchen door. He heard her Camry fire up in the driveway and then drive off, leaving him alone with his thoughts. He left the omelet on the table and took his coffee outside to the patio.

Sitting on his bench, he reflected on what Estelle had said. Maybe she was right. Once he saw the dead baby, life to death, he tried to outrun the sight of his face on the dead baby, but he couldn't outrun his own mortality—or even the knowledge of his own mortality. Something like that.

Fernando went back into the kitchen and ate his omelet with a second cup of coffee. After a third cup, he went into his study and checked his iphone for messages. Nothing from Manny so far this morning.

Fernando had stopped by Manny's office at the Washington Avenue Station on his way home yesterday afternoon and played the recording for him. Manny, a smart-ass technology wizard, showed him how to send a Voice Memos file by email. For whatever incomprehensible reason Fernando still had a hard time transferring the file, so Manny grabbed Fernando's iphone and did it himself, sending the file to his office computer for storage.

Fernando recalled Manny saying he would put out an APB on Joey Alhambra this morning. That meant Antonio would no longer be the number one suspect in the murder of Chris Chabot. He'd called Antonio to tell him the news when he finally made it home last night. This time Antonio's phone was turned on, but he didn't answer. So Fernando had left him a message.

While he brooded in his study, he heard his phone ping. He checked the screen and found a text from Antonio:

"Thanks for the news, but I'm not convinced I'm off the hook just yet. I'm still a suspect. Fuckers!"

After checking his email and finding nothing from Manny or Antonio or anyone else he was waiting to hear from, Fernando sat back in his chair and cursed. What was he doing? Time to step back. Time to relax. Why did he keep taking on these cases that weren't even cases, because he wasn't getting paid? Not only that, but he hadn't been asked to get involved. Manny had merely told him to warn Antonio, as he recalled. Nothing more.

Fernando decided to do something he hadn't done in more than twenty years. He went directly to the bedroom and dressed in chinos and a button-down shirt. He even slipped into a pair of dress shoes, not his usual hiking boots. Then he went into the bathroom and washed his face and combed his hair, breaking his rule to never look into the mirror.

Minutes later he locked the house and climbed into his Cherokee. He drove down to the Paseo and around to Alameda Street, where he turned into the big parking lot. He hurried, not wanting to be late. By the time he walked up the steps to the Cathedral Basilica of Saint Francis the music had already started. He passed by the three statues in front of the cathedral—Saint Francis of Assisi, Archbishop Jean-Baptiste Lamy, and Kateri Tekakwitha—and walked through the massive doors and into the nave.

Inside he stopped for a moment and studied the beautiful interior of the cathedral, with granite pillars on each side and rows of benches leading down to the sanctuary and its altar screen, a hand-carved wooden reredos showing an 18th century statue of Saint Francis surrounded by painted images of New World saints. The soft brown wood and the golden backgrounds of the various figures glowed brightly in the morning light. A place of peace and contemplation.

Curious, but he felt at ease here, which surprised Fernando, given his break with the church. Then he spotted Estelle halfway down the rows sitting with Dorothy Rodriguez, the widow of his best friend Fidel Rodriguez, a former reporter for the *Independent*, who'd been murdered last year while doing a story on the witchcraft murderer. He took a seat on the bench next to Estelle.

Surprised, Estelle whispered, "What are you doing here?"

"I came to be with you," Fernando said. "I don't know, maybe we can spend the day together."

Estelle raised her eyebrows and then smiled, sort of. "Okay."

After mass they drove home in their separate vehicles. They ate a light lunch and then decided to do something they hadn't done in years: hike the Aspen Vista Trail on the road to the Santa Fe Ski Basin. Estelle refused to ride in the Cherokee, so they took her Camry.

Fernando didn't mind riding in the Camry, except for the fact that Estelle drove at least five miles per hour under the speed limit. Like a snail. He bit his tongue, trying not to complain. He told himself to relax and enjoy the spectacular scenery as they drove up Hyde Park Road into the Sangre de Cristo Mountains. The aspens hadn't yet turned. In a couple of weeks the forest would be a sea of flaming yellow aspen leaves among the green Ponderosa pines. They parked in the lot near the Aspen Vista trailhead and spent the afternoon alternately hiking and resting in the meadows they encountered along the trail.

The sun was already starting to set when they drove back down Hyde Park Road to the city. Instead of going directly home, they decided to stop at La Choza for dinner. They didn't get home until half past eight o'clock.

It was the most relaxing day Fernando had spent in years.

## 26

Next morning Fernando woke up feeling more refreshed than he'd felt in days, maybe weeks. For the first time all week he hadn't been tormented by his nightmare of being trapped in a dark house with a weeping woman and a slap in the face called mortality. Taking the day off from his usual routine had worked its magic. He felt renewed, so much so that he considered taking another day off and going fishing with one of his fishing buddies. Then he remembered that none of them would be available. Fidel was dead, Manny was working, and Antonio was still hiding in the Pecos, as far as he knew.

Considering his options, Fernando dressed quickly and made himself a light breakfast of fruit and toast. Estelle had left for work earlier, so he finished cleaning up the kitchen, washing and putting away their dishes. He made himself a final cup of coffee and took it and his cell phone out to the patio. As always, his first instinct was to check for email on his cell phone, but today he waited until he'd finished his cup of coffee. When he picked it up, the screen blinked on and Antonio's name appeared as the phone began to ring. An ingrained sense of duty made him click the accept icon.

"Fernando, I got them in my sights, both of them," Antonio announced. "Ziggy and Alhambra."

"How? Where?" Fernando asked, not happy that he was about to be dragged into this mess again.

"I've been following Ziggy every time he leaves Rancho Nirvana," Antonio said. "This morning I followed him all the way to Taos. He went to meet Alhambra at the El Pueblo Lodge. I saw him pull into the lodge and park next to Alhambra's Escalade. I'm across the street in the parking lot of the abandoned Kachina Lodge. You remember the El Pueblo. We stayed there on a couple of cases."

Fernando did indeed remember the El Pueblo. He'd stayed there several times, most recently on his Taos Vendetta case. A small, 1960s-style motel where guests could park in front of their rooms, the El Pueblo consisted of two shotgun buildings facing each other across the parking lot. The El Pueblo had seen better days, which made it a perfect place to keep out of sight. Its faux adobe buildings dated from a different era, before the age of gentrification produced expensive resorts and 'boutique' hotels like those that blighted Santa Fe.

"So what do you intend to do?" Fernando asked.

"Not sure. I might wait until I get them one on one, or I might just go in solo and clean house," Antonio said.

Fernando sighed. "Bad idea. You need back up. Wait until I get there before you do anything, okay?"

"So you're coming up, then?" Antonio asked.

"I'm on my way," Fernando said and clicked off, cursing. What choice did he have anyway? He couldn't abandon Antonio now.

Not what he expected to do today, but so what? He knew from experience that expectations were just that: expectations. Meant nothing.

Fernando went inside and finished dressing. He left a hand-written note on the kitchen table for Estelle, apologizing for his absence and explaining why he had to go up to Taos. Then he went into his study to get the holster carrying his Smith & Wesson and locked the house.

He deposited his Smith & Wesson in the glove compartment and then fired up the Cherokee, driving around the Paseo to the Highway 84/285 ramp and taking off fast, speeding past the Santa Fe Opera and the Tesuque turnoff. He had to slow down entering the Pojoaque commercial corridor and then hit the gas hard once past the old Line Camp and the turnoff to Los Alamos. By the time he cleared junky Española on Highway 68 he began to relax. Driving alongside the Rio Grande always made him reflective, with the hills and then the cliffs on both sides of the river suffused with the bright New Mexico light.

Fernando kept thinking that if his friend Hank Mathews had not retired as the head of the Taos Police Department, he would call old Hank and ask for help. But Hank had retired a couple of years ago and Chris Perez had taken over as head. He didn't know Chris nearly as well and didn't feel comfortable asking him for help until he knew more about the situation.

He passed through Ranchos de Taos, getting a brief look at San Francisco de Assis, the famous catholic church that had been immortalized by many artists, including Georgia O'Keeffe and Ansell Adams. Then past the Sagebrush Inn and into downtown Taos on what they called the Paseo del Pueblo Sud, which became Paseo del Pueblo Norte once past the Plaza area. El Pueblo Lodge was a couple of blocks north of the Plaza on the left side of the Paseo.

Fernando bypassed El Pueblo and turned right into the large parking lot of the Kachina Lodge, which had been closed for months, if not years. He had no idea if the owners were going to sell or remodel the historic lodge, just south of the famous Taos Pueblo, a UNESCO World Heritage Site. Looked like some of the rooms had been vandalized by vagrants or hooligans. Broken windows, old furniture tossed outside on the sidewalk. Since the last time he'd been in this part of town, the neglected lodge had become an eyesore.

At first Fernando didn't see Antonio. He drove further into the expansive parking lot before finding Antonio's Wrangler behind a stand of trees on the left side of the lot. Antonio sat in front of the Wrangler in a folding camp chair looking as relaxed as if he were camping in the national forest. A pair of binoculars hung from his neck. The big man stepped out of the trees and flagged him down.

Fernando parked behind the main office building, where his Cherokee couldn't be seen from the Paseo, and walked across the lot to join Antonio.

"Good to see you," Antonio said. "I thought I might have to do this myself."

Fernando shook his head. "Slow down. This isn't going to be easy."

"What do you mean?" Antonio protested.

"I mean you can't just walk into a public motel with your guns blazing," Fernando said, exasperated by having to explain. "First of all, you could end up killing innocent bystanders. Second, this is a job for law enforcement. Let me call Manny and see how he wants to play this."

Not happy, Antonio threw up his arms. "Okay, call."

Fernando leaned against the Wrangler and took his cell phone out of his pocket. He scrolled down the list of recent calls and clicked on Manny's number. Manny, always punctual, answered immediately.

"Fernando...what now?" Manny asked, sounding a bit apprehensive, as if he expected bad news.

"Manny, I'm in Taos with Antonio," Fernando said. "We found Ziggy and Alhambra. They're staying at the El Pueblo Lodge. We're across the street at the Kachina. What do you want us to do?"

"Are you sure it's them?" Manny asked.

"Yes, both their cars are parked outside one of the rooms, a black Escalade and a green Subaru Outback."

"Okay...stay put. I'll call Chris Perez, the new chief of the Taos Police Department," Manny said and clicked off.

Fernando noticed Antonio gesturing wildly in the direction of the El Pueblo Lodge. He immediately saw why. Ziggy and Alhambra had come out of their room and were walking down the sidewalk to the Paseo. They turned right and headed down the street. Two doors down they stopped in front of Michael's Kitchen, one of the most popular restaurants in Taos. Ziggy opened the door and the two of them disappeared inside the restaurant.

Fernando checked his watch. Almost Noon.

"Must be going for lunch," Antonio said.

"Yeah. I wish I were going for lunch," Fernando replied.

Antonio shrugged. "So what did Manny say?"

"He's calling in the Taos Police," Fernando said. "He wants us to stay put and let them take over."

Antonio frowned. Clearly he was not happy that they were being called off. For years Antonio had been the enforcer at the Santa Fe Police Department. It wasn't easy for him to step back and let others do the enforcing. He liked nothing better than to see heads roll.

So they waited, waited for Ziggy and Alhambra to come out of Michael's Kitchen and for the Taos Police to arrive at the El Pueblo. About thirty minutes later Ziggy and Alhambra left Michael's Kitchen and walked back to their room. From a distance their talking seemed animated as if they were arguing. They quickly disappeared into their room.

While Fernando and Antonio watched from the Kachina, a couple of other guests left their rooms and went into the office to check out. Then after stopping in their rooms to get their suitcases, they drove out of the El Pueblo parking lot and disappeared on the Paseo.

Moments later Fernando spotted a Taos Police Department cruiser turning into the El Pueblo parking lot. The cruiser slowed as it made the rounds looking for the Escalade and the Outback. Two cops rode in the cruiser, the driver and another sitting in the passenger's seat holding what looked like a shotgun. The cruiser hesitated for a moment as it approached the two vehicles parked side by side in front of the room, the Escalade first and then the Outback. Finally the cruiser pulled in on the other side of the Outback and came to an abrupt stop.

Even from afar Fernando felt the tension. It was show time.

# 27

Fernando and Antonio watched the scene unfold.

The officer in the driver's seat got out of the cruiser and walked up to the door of the room where Alhambra was staying. The other officer holding the shotgun opened his door and sat in the passenger's seat, ready.

The lead officer knocked on the door with a long nightstick and then stepped back. For a split second all action seemed to freeze. Suddenly the door swung open revealing Ziggy and Alhambra. Both carried pistols.

The officer started to say something, but before he could Alhambra raised his pistol and opened fire, all in a split second. The officer staggered back from the door and then fell on the sidewalk, his head bouncing on the concrete.

Then Ziggy ran out of the room with his gun blazing. His bullets shattered the window of the cruiser.

Ducking, the officer in the passenger's seat squeezed out of the cruiser with his shotgun. He squatted down on one knee and pulled the trigger of the shotgun. The loud blast knocked Ziggy off his feet. He fell back in the doorway of the room.

The officer turned his shotgun to Alhambra, but Alhambra shot first. And shot again and again until the officer crumpled up in a heap on the concrete parking lot.

Alhambra didn't waste any time. He went over to check Ziggy and then ran back into the room. Moments later he reappeared, carrying two suitcases, which he tossed in the rear of the Escalade. Then he gunned the big motor, backed up fast, and squealed out of the parking lot. He turned north on the Paseo and disappeared around the big curve near the turnoff to Taos Pueblo.

"Let's go after him," Antonio said, climbing into his Wrangler.

"No, you follow him and let me know where he lands," Fernando replied. "I need to stay here and tell the cops what happened. I'll call Chris Perez right now."

"Suit yourself," Antonio said, driving off quickly. He turned right on the Paseo and followed Alhambra.

Alone, Fernando clicked on the phone number of the Taos Police Department, which he still had on his phone from previous cases. "This is Fernando Lopez...I'm calling Chief Perez to report three homicides at the El Pueblo Lodge," he said to the receptionist, who put him through to Perez.

"Fernando?" the Chief came on line.

"Hi Chris," Fernando answered. "I don't know if you remember me, I'm a friend of Hank Mathews. We worked on many cases together."

"Of course I remember you," Perez shot back. "Old Hank talked about you all the time. So what's this about three homicides at the El Pueblo?"

Fernando briefly explained what had happened and that the one shooter who got away was extremely dangerous. "Joey Alhambra—Manny sent out an APB on him either yesterday or this morning."

"Yeah, it came in this morning," Perez said, sighing. "This is the last thing I wanted to hear."

Fernando didn't know what to say. Apologize?

"Okay, thanks, I'll send a car right over and notify Forensics," Perez said, clicking off.

Fernando climbed into his Cherokee and drove across the street to the El Pueblo Lodge parking lot. He made sure to park far away from the damaged police cruiser and the three bodies.

When he stepped out of the Cherokee, he noticed a crowd of gawkers had assembled over by the crime scene. Several couples, even a few kids, stood staring at the grisly sight. He walked in front of them and said, "Move back, please. This is a crime scene. The Taos police are on the way."

The crowd moved back. They began to disperse when they heard the police siren blaring down the Paseo.

The police car roared into the parking lot and pulled up parallel to the crime scene, blocking the area from unwanted spectators. Two older officers jumped out and stopped dead in their tracks when they spotted the three bodies sprawled over the terrain, the two officers outside on the sidewalk and in the parking lot and one civilian lying just inside the open door of the motel room.

The bigger of the two officers cursed as he bent down to examine the officer lying in the parking lot next to the shotgun. Then he moved up to the sidewalk where his other colleague had fallen, still clinging to his nightstick.

The second officer, whose nametag read 'Jerry Romero,' came over to Fernando. "Are you Lopez?"

Fernando nodded. "Yeah, I called in the shooting. I'm a former detective on the Santa Fe Police Department. I've been tracking the shooter here, Joey Alhambra. An APB went out this morning. He's extremely dangerous."

Jerry looked at the grisly scene. "I guess so. So who's this other guy in the doorway Bob's looking at?"

"His name is Frank Tate, although he goes by Ziggy," Fernando said. "He and Alhambra sell drugs."

By this time Bob, the older officer, was on his knees examining the body of Ziggy, whose chest looked like a spongy mass of blood. "I'll be damned. He looks like a hippie version of that Wild West figure. What was his name?"

"Buffalo Bill," Fernando responded.

"That's it! That's the one. Looks like the shotgun tore him up pretty good," Bob said. "He won't be selling any more drugs."

While they talked, a Forensics van pulled into the lot and parked behind the cruiser. Two men climbed out of the van and walked over to Jerry and Bob.

Fernando moved aside, so the crew could begin their work. He found a patio table on the far side of the parking lot near the El Pueblo office. From there he watched the Forensics boys photograph and collect evidence, which they carefully placed in plastic bags and sealed.

Fernando noticed a woman, one of the El Pueblo desk clerks, standing in the doorway watching the crime scene. She came over to his table with an unhappy look on her face.

"Aiiieee, this is not good for business," she said, a middle-aged woman with dark curly hair wearing jeans and a sweater. "All our guests are leaving—and who's gonna come tonight with this going on?"

"I sympathize with you, but they're working as fast as they can," Fernando said. "The guy who rented the room is a mass murderer. It's important to collect all the evidence."

The woman did not respond. Instead, she lingered in silence for a while and then wandered back into the office.

Eventually Jerry came over to the table and sat across from Fernando. "I need to get your statement," he said, taking out his notebook.

Introducing himself, Fernando explained what he and Antonio

were doing here and described what they had seen from where they were positioned across the Paseo at the Kachina. He described the shooting in great detail, including how Alhambra had made his escape after shooting the second officer.

"The officers never had a chance," Fernando said. "Alhambra and Ziggy opened fire immediately."

When the interview was finished, Fernando and Jerry sat at the table and watched while Bob helped with the cleanup.

Overhead a neon sign blinked on and off in the dying afternoon light.

# 28

Two hours later Fernando watched the Forensics van drive out of the parking lot. The Forensics crew had sealed Alhambra's room and left a small area in front cordoned off with yellow tape, which meant they would be back. Meanwhile he'd been waiting to hear from Antonio. He had no idea where Antonio and Alhambra were or what had transpired between them.

Fernando checked the time. Almost four o'clock. He hadn't eaten lunch today, so he decided to walk over to Michael's Kitchen for a late lunch/early dinner. Then he remembered that Michael's closed at two in the afternoon. So he decided to drive to the Sagebrush Inn. The Sagebrush Grill had a tasty breakfast burrito that was available all day, as he recalled.

That settled, he climbed into his Cherokee and drove south through downtown Taos to the Sagebrush Inn and pulled into a parking space near the front entrance of the hundred-year-old adobe building. With the ends of its interior vigas protruding from its brown stucco walls, and with heavy wooden doors and window frames, the historic Sagebrush looked more like a frontier fort than an inn.

Fernando set the brake and climbed out of his Cherokee, stepping into the spacious lobby that always made him feel like stepping back in time. The interior of the hotel was classic Taos: thick adobe walls with a rough coating of stucco, exposed vigas on the ceiling, and various Southwestern antiques hanging on the walls, along with stuffed animal heads and paintings of famous Native Americans and Taoseños. Resembled a damn Wild West museum.

Fernando ignored the Cantina to his left, although he was tempted, and turned right into the Grill. The long rectangular room had exposed vigas on the ceiling, dark clunky tables and chairs, and an adobe partial wall that for some reason was painted midnight blue. He sat at a corner table looking out at the patio and waited for the lone server to notice him. The young man was reading a newspaper on the counter and couldn't be bothered.

"Afternoon," Fernando said loudly, to get the server's attention.

"Oh, hello," the server said. He grabbed a menu and brought it over to Fernando's table.

"Can I still get the breakfast burrito with red chile?" Fernando asked.

"Sure thing. Something to drink with that?"

"Modelo, please," Fernando said.

The server wrote down the order and took it to the kitchen. Minutes later he reappeared with the Modelo and then the burrito. Starving, Fernando ate like a hungry wolf, devouring the large burrito quickly. He was working on finishing the Modelo when his cell phone rang.

"Antonio...I've been waiting for your call," Fernando answered.

"I got the motherfucker treed," Antonio replied. "I followed him up Highway five-twenty-two around to Red River. He stopped at the Best Western Rivers Edge on River Street. It's right on the Red River. My guess is that tomorrow he's either headed north into Colorado or cutting over to Interstate Twenty-Five down to Albuquerque or El Paso. Maybe Juarez."

"Makes sense," Fernando said. "So where can I find you? Are you at the Best Western now?"

"Yeah, I'm in back near the river on the eastern side of the building. You'll find me sitting at a picnic table in a stand of trees."

"Okay, Red River's only about forty miles away," Fernando said. "I should be there in forty-five minutes or so."

Antonio clicked off.

Fernando left a couple of twenty dollar bills on the table and then walked out of the Sagebrush and climbed into his Cherokee. Taking his time, he drove back through Taos and followed scenic Highway 522, one of his favorite highways. Along the way he passed the turnoff to the D. H. Lawrence Ranch, where the English writer had lived for a short time back in the 1920s. Just past San Cristobal he saw Wild Rivers National Recreation Area off to the left, a pristine camping and fishing area with miles of hiking trails. At Questa he turned right on Highway 38 and entered the Carson National Forest with its 12,000-foot mountains towering in the distance. The town of Red River was a few miles up the highway on its namesake river.

Red River was both a tiny cowboy town and a skiing town for those who did not want to attempt the more challenging peaks of the nearby Taos Ski Basin. The highway ran alongside the river, named after the red clay soil and silt that muddied the water. Coming into town Fernando saw the Best Western Rivers Edge straight ahead on his right. A piney, shotgun-style Western lodge with wooden balconies overlooking the river in back, the two-story lodge resembled a thousand other motels scattered throughout the West. Except for the river, which gave it a special feel, like a mountain lodge in a national forest.

Fernando saw that the parking lot was completely full when he turned off the highway. He spotted Antonio's Wrangler parked on the eastern side of the lot. Alhambra's Escalade was parked more toward the western side. Taking a chance, he pulled over on a patch of gravel next to Antonio's Wrangler. He debated whether he should get his Smith & Wesson out of the glove compartment. Finally he grabbed the holster and took it with him outside, where he buckled up. Better to be prepared than sorry. He'd already seen Alhambra in action once, so he knew the pusher man was packing.

Locking the Cherokee, he noticed the day had turned unseasonably cool—and dark. The sun had set low in the western sky. That and the thick gray clouds coming in from the north had muted what was left of the sun. Moving into the shadows, he crept through the trees around to the eastern side of the lodge. He tried his best not to make any noise. He was looking for the picnic table that Antonio had staked out as he moved through the trees that ran between the lodge and the river. Up ahead he saw lights now, flickering from the rear balconies of the rooms that overlooked the river. Then he heard voices. It turned out a group of four or five people were talking and laughing as they walked along the river, which through the scattered trees looked like a black slash in the otherwise gray gloom.

Easing out from the protection of the trees, Fernando spotted a picnic table in the shadows. A hulking figure sat at the table staring at the rear of the lodge. "Antonio?" he whispered.

The hulking figure turned in Fernando's direction. "Over here at the table. Have a seat."

Fernando shuffled over to the table and sat down.

"Alhambra's in the third unit down on the lower level," Antonio said, pointing at the lodge, where long wooden balconies on both levels ran the length of the building, which looked almost hazy in the gathering dusk. "I saw Alhambra out on the balcony earlier drinking a beer."

Fernando looked at the third door down. Curtains were drawn tight over the double window accessing the balcony. A wrought iron table and chairs stood in front of this room and all the others.

"What's your plan?" Fernando asked, getting nervous.

"We grab him when he comes out," Antonio said. "If he doesn't come out, we go in after dark and grab him. I'll handcuff him and call the State Police."

Noticing Antonio wasn't wearing his gun, Fernando asked, "You're not armed?"

"I won't need it. Trust me."

Just then Alhambra opened his door and stepped out on the balcony.

# 29

Alhambra walked across the wooden balcony to the guardrail. Looking out over the river, he rested his hands on the top rail. Then he turned and walked to the side stairway at the very end of the balcony. He descended slowly in the dim light and then walked down through the trees to the riverbank and stood at river's edge. Taking his time now, he meandered down along the river stopping every few feet to study the river, as if looking for something, fish maybe.

Suddenly a bolt of lightning illuminated the grounds like a flashbulb, followed by thunder that cracked open the sky. Alhambra jumped but then steadied himself and looked up at the sky. While he gazed skyward a light, gentle rain started to fall out of the dark sky.

"Okay, let's move," Antonio said. "You go down to the river and follow him. I'll go down through the trees and come around in front of him. When you hear me whistle, make yourself seen by Alhambra. I'll do the rest."

Fernando felt dubious about Antonio's plan, if you could call it a plan. They didn't know the layout here or what they would find along the river. Not to mention the obvious omission: what would they do with Alhambra when they caught up with him?

Still, Fernando wanted to avoid sounding cowardly, so he waited until Antonio got up from the picnic table and walked along the trees parallel to the river until he was almost out of sight. When Antonio finally disappeared into the trees, Fernando moved out quickly. He entered the trees and walked down toward the river, where he found a well-used dirt path that ran through the trees along the riverbank, about ten yards from the river.

Fernando continued walking along the path that followed the river. He had no idea where either Alhambra or Antonio were located. Somewhere up ahead.

Soon the rain began to pick up, beginning to soak his clothing as he walked. Again he heard thunder rumbling angrily overhead, but no lightning. On he walked, peering into the gloomy gray light for any sign of Alhambra.

Walking more cautiously now, Fernando imagined Alhambra hiding behind every tree, every shadow. Where was Antonio? He would feel more comfortable if he knew Antonio was nearby.

Just then he heard Antonio whistle. At least he thought it was Antonio and not a bird. Birds didn't sing in the rain, did they? He decided to take a chance.

Following Antonio's plan, Fernando moved out of the trees down to the river. He looked desperately for Alhambra but saw no one, only the shadows of the trees along the river and the streaks of rain falling.

Then he made a misstep. Coming too close to the river, he slipped on the wet, muddy bank. Next thing Fernando knew he was sliding into the dark river. He tried to grab onto something on the bank to stop his fall but only came up with a handful of sticky mud.

"Fuck!" he cursed, flailing about in the cold water.

Suddenly he spotted Alhambra, who'd stuck his head out of the trees to see what was going on. "Stop!" he yelled at Alhambra.

"What?" Alhambra said and moved closer to the river. He took a pistol out from under his jacket and took a step forward. "Who's there?"

At that exact moment Antonio came roaring out of the trees and tackled Alhambra before the pusher man could get off a clear shot. Alhambra's pistol exploded as the two plunged into the river, arms wrapped around each other.

Then the real fight began. Alhambra tried to hit Antonio with his pistol, but Antonio knocked the pistol out of his hand. The two men thrashed about in the water, wrestling and cursing at each other.

Fernando tried his best to reach them. He sloshed through the murky, waist-high water drenched from head to foot. His wet clothing felt as heavy as cement wrapped around him.

Up ahead in the river the two men continued to wrestle. Alhambra was tough, but he was no match for Antonio who was half a foot taller and outweighed him buy at least fifty pounds. It took Antonio only a few minutes to subdue Alhambra, choking him from behind and then holding his head under water.

When provoked, Antonio was like a raging beast. Fernando had seen him in action many times when they had worked together in their years at the Santa Fe Police Department. Fernando had never seen anyone get the better of Antonio. He was simply too big, too powerful.

The only noise now was Antonio plunging Alhambra's body into the water, again and again. Finally he held Alhambra under the water for several minutes, all the while making a growling noise.

Fernando stopped about ten yards from Antonio. "Be careful, you'll kill him."

Antonio looked up at him and snarled. "He was a dead man the moment I saw him in the trees."

With that, Antonio reached underwater and grabbed one of Alhambra's feet. Then he dragged the body face down out of the river and up on the bank, dropping the foot unceremoniously and brushed off his hands.

Fernando and Antonio looked at each other and burst out laughing.

"Jesus, Antonio, you look like a drowned rat," Fernando said.

"Yeah, well, you don't look much better," Antonio replied.

Antonio was holding his left arm right below the shoulder. "What's wrong with your arm?" Fernando asked.

"Stings like a motherfucker," Antonio said.

Noticing a rip in Antonio's shirt, Fernando examined the big man's shoulder and found blood oozing out of a nasty wound. "Looks like a bullet...flesh wound. It missed the bone."

"Fucker shot me," Antonio said.

"Well, he won't be shooting anyone else."

Suddenly Antonio turned and motioned toward the lodge. "Looks like we have company."

A tall man wearing a leather vest came marching down the riverbank toward them. Several others stood on the balcony gawking at them. Without knowing it, they'd drawn a crowd.

"What in the hell is going on down here?" the man in the vest asked. "I'm the manager here."

Antonio stepped forward and looked down at him. "We're police from Santa Fe. This man is a mass murderer. We've been chasing him for days and finally caught up with him here. I want you to call State Police immediately and alert them. They'll need to send a body back to Santa Fe. Understand what I'm saying?"

The man stepped back. "A mass murderer? Good God. That's all we need here."

"Call the State Police," Antonio repeated. "And get rid of the peanut gallery up there. We don't need an audience."

The man nodded and hurried off, shooing the onlookers back into their rooms.

Fernando smiled at Antonio. "A slight exaggeration...."

"Stick to the story," Antonio said. "No harm, no foul."

## 30

Several days later Fernando was enjoying a late morning walk along Acequia Madre Street. Since returning from Red River, he'd been sticking close to home and trying to relax. Antonio's ruse had worked with the State Police when they arrived at the Best Western Rivers Edge. Even though the two officers seemed dubious of Antonio's story, they finally capitulated. Antonio, given his size and intensity, had that effect on people. The officers made arrangements for an ambulance to take Joey Alhambra's body and his Escalade back to Santa Fe where Manny and the Santa Fe Police Department took over the case.

As he walked along the picturesque street of million-dollar remodeled adobes and colorful gardens Fernando became aware of a vehicle following along behind him. Stopping, he turned to see Antonio's blue Wrangler.

"Get in—you can buy me lunch at the Shed," Antonio yelled, after buzzing down the front passenger's side window.

Fernando checked the time. Quarter past eleven. That meant the Shed would be open for business. So he climbed into the Wrangler and buckled his seat belt. He noticed a pile of suitcases and duffle bags in the rear. Was Antonio going somewhere?

"I wonder how many lunches at the Shed I've bought you over the years," Fernando mused.

Antonio laughed. "I have some news. I'll make it worth your while."

With that, Antonio negotiated a wide U-turn, not easy on narrow Acequia Madre Street. He drove over the sidewalk on the other side of the road and side-swiped an unfortunate cherry tree before righting the Wrangler and cruising down to the Paseo. He drove around the Paseo to Marcy Street and turned left, finding a parking space on the street next to the coffee shop.

Fernando was eager to hear Antonio's news but decided to wait until they were seated at the restaurant. They walked down Washington Avenue to East Palace Avenue and then a half block up to The Shed. The Shed's remodeled but still funky exterior greeted them with its smorgasbord of bright colors—mostly blue, red, and purple. Inside was more sedate, a classy mixture of beige and browns. After they were seated at a corner table, a server quickly appeared. No time to waste, because the Shed was one of the busiest restaurants in the city.

"I'll have the chicken enchilada plate with red chile," Fernando told the server, a young woman with flaming red hair and freckles.

"Ditto," Antonio added. "And two Modelo drafts."

"Why do all the young women wear nose rings and/or color their hair red or blue these days?" Fernando asked, after the young woman walked away with their orders. "Do they think that's attractive? Appealing? Sexy? What?"

Antonio shrugged. "It's a fad. Like tattoos. No big deal."

Moments later another server brought their drinks. The Shed knew how to get people in and out fast.

Antonio raised his glass and said, "Cheers."

They tapped glasses.

"I feel like they have us on a clock," Fernando said. "It's a helluva way to enjoy a meal."

Antonio shrugged. "Life in a tourist town."

"So what's your news? Enough of the suspense."

Antonio took a long drink. "Okay, some of this is gonna be new to you. A lot of it, in fact. First, I have a son who just turned twenty. You know about my marriage and my ex-wife. Our marriage ended because I couldn't control my Post Traumatic Stress Syndrome...which by the way seems to have improved, at least for the moment. I think this episode with Chabot's murder and chasing Alhambra gave me the jolt I needed to move beyond my anxiety, like the old-fashioned shock treatment doctors used to treat depression. Kind of like a computer reboot."

Fernando was shocked. "A son? Jesus, Antonio, why didn't you ever tell me?"

Antonio shrugged. "I don't know. Just didn't know how to bring it up, I guess. Anyway, even though my marriage ended, I've always managed to keep in touch, seeing him on birthdays and holidays and so forth. Well, he just inherited his maternal grandmother's ranch in southern Colorado, not far from Alamosa. That is, my ex-wife's mother—her father died years ago—left the ranch to our son, Billy. Billy asked me to come up and help him run the ranch, at least temporarily. So, to make a long story short, I'm on my way to Colorado now. I kept my cabin in the Pecos, in case I want to come here for vacations or maybe even move back to New Mexico some day. You never know what the future will bring."

Fernando shook his head. He didn't want to believe Antonio was leaving.

"So let's call this a see-you-later, not a goodbye," Antonio said. "I'll be back, and you'll be the first to know."

Fernando was stunned. He and Antonio had been best friends for years. He couldn't count the cases they'd been on together at the Santa Fe Police Department and even later when he'd been a private investigator.

"I don't know what to say," Fernando mumbled finally.

"You could wish my son and I good luck, for starters," Antonio said.

"Of course I wish you good luck! But damn, what am I gonna do without you to bail me out of tight situations?"

Antonio laughed, sort of, just as their food arrived.

They ate in silence, both of them somber.

When he finished eating, Fernando pushed aside his plate and sat back in his chair. "What about this Chris Chabot affair?"

Antonio shook his head. "Manny knows how to reach me if he needs to. Shouldn't be necessary now, after they found the wire garrote in Ziggy's barn. Their DNA was all over it, Ziggy's and Alhambra's."

Fernando nodded. After he paid the bill they walked back to Antonio's Wrangler in silence. When Antonio dropped him off at his house, both got out and hugged each other for a few moments and then said goodbye. They would keep in touch, all the bullshit things people say to each other before they part when they suspect they will never see each other again.

Fernando watched Antonio drive off and turn left on Acequia Madre, out of his life. He felt numb, overwhelmed by an incredible sadness.

He walked to the kitchen door and stepped inside, brewing himself a cup of coffee in the Keurig and sitting at the kitchen table. After he finished, he didn't know what to do with himself. He went into his study and sat at his desk for a while, staring at a blank computer screen on his laptop. Then he went into the living room and picked up a book, any book he could find on the coffee table, but was unable to concentrate on what he was reading. After a couple of hours, he gave up. The house felt so lonesome with Estelle at work and the thought of never seeing Antonio again that he decided to go visit Ruby at her gallery on Canyon Road. Ruby could always cheer him up, even in his darkest moments.

Fernando locked the house and climbed into his Cherokee. Once on the Paseo he drove quickly around to Canyon Road and pulled into the parking lot beside Ruby's gallery. He saw his old office, idle now that he had closed his private eye business, another casualty of time. Inside Ruby was standing at the front counter looking over a computer printout.

"Hey, Fernando," she said, removing her reading glasses and tossing them on the counter.

"What's up?" he asked. "You don't look so happy."

"Business sucks, that's what's up," Ruby said, brushing her long black hair out of her eyes. "I need some commercial shit to sell in here, something that tourists will actually buy."

Fernando laughed. "Good luck with that."

"Say, you'll never guess who just stopped by to chat," Ruby said. "Lulu, Ziggy's wife. I don't know if you remember her. She and Ziggy married some forty years ago when they were hippie stoners. Seems they didn't bother to get divorced when Lulu split for Oregon not long after they were married. They were a couple of acid heads back then."

"Long blond hair? Spaced-out?" Fernando asked. "I sort of remember her."

"That's her," Ruby replied. "Now she's back claiming to be the new owner of Rancho Nirvana. She showed me their wedding certificate, so she's legit, but I don't know why anyone would want that shit-hole."

"Well, the land would be worth a lot."

"Yeah, maybe, if you burned down all the buildings," Ruby shot back. She tossed the computer printout on the counter with her glasses. "Oh hell, let's go to El Farol for Happy Hour. It's time to get happy."

"I can't argue with that, I just lost my best friend," Fernando replied.

Ruby stared at him, waiting for an explanation.

## 31

On their walk down Canyon Road to El Farol Fernando told Ruby about Antonio's decision to leave New Mexico. That Antonio was moving to Alamosa, Colorado, to help his twenty-year-old son Billy run a ranch that Billy had inherited from his maternal grandmother. And that Antonio would keep his cabin in the Pecos Wilderness, just in case he wanted to return for vacations or whatever.

"Son? I didn't know Antonio had a son," Ruby said. "Hard to imagine that big gorilla as a father, especially since he's had a history of dealing with PTSD. I mean, the guy can be a brute."

"I didn't know either," Fernando said. "Antonio kept it on the downlow. He said he saw his son only on birthdays and holidays."

"And what does Antonio know about running a ranch?" Ruby asked. "I mean, he's been a Marine or a cop for his entire adult life, neither of which prepare you to raise cows and horses or whatever the hell ranchers do."

"No idea," Fernando replied.

"Yeah, it kinda makes you wonder what else we don't know about him—he was always so damn secretive, if you know what I mean," Ruby said, as they approached El Farol. They climbed the steps to the long porch in front and stepped inside the venerable restaurant.

The bar part was crowded with old timers, artists mostly, arguing about one thing or another. Fernando followed Ruby into the restaurant part of La Fonda. They liked to sit at a table near the colorful Flamenco mural on the wall. They were the first of their usual group to arrive today.

"Tessa's running late, but she should be here soon," Ruby said, sitting down at the table.

Fernando sat beside her, placing his cell phone on the table in front of him.

They ordered their usual: margarita for Ruby, Modelo draft for Fernando.

Just as the server delivered their beverages, Tessa and Blaine burst through the front door. As usual, they seemed to be quarreling about something.

"What's the problem now?" Ruby asked her younger sister.

"Blaine won't take me on a honeymoon," Tessa said, sitting across the table from Ruby and giving Blaine a dirty look.

Ruby, choking on her margarita, sputtered, "What? You got married?"

"Yep, I made an honest woman out of her," Blaine joked.

"We just came from City Hall. Here's the marriage certificate," Tessa said, plopping the paper down on the table. "I think I made a mistake. Is there a five-day return period or what?"

"I told you not to marry that miscreant, but you never listen to me, sis," Ruby said. "This guy's just as much of a womanizer as your first husband."

"Yeah, well, monogamy was never your strong point either, as I recall," Tessa shot back.

Before they could continue, Fernando stood up and waved his hands. "Stop it! I have some real news. Antonio's leaving town."

"No way...." Blaine muttered.

Fernando explained why Antonio was leaving and that he may or may not return for a visit in the future. While he did, the server brought Tessa and Blaine margaritas. Tessa waited for Fernando to finish, Blaine didn't.

"Hah! I suspected he had a secret life," Blaine said, after a long drink of his margarita. "Living out there in that primitive cabin...something had to be wrong with him."

"Hey—show some respect," Ruby said. "We've lost too many friends lately. "Raoul Garcia's dead, so is Fidel Rodriguez, Wayne Fontenot, Andy Dejon, Jimmy Mackey, and even crazy Ziggy. Now Antonio's leaving us. Our ranks are thinning out. Our entire generation is passing. Wake up!"

Fernando nodded. "I miss them too, all of them. When Antonio told me he was leaving, I felt lost, abandoned. I've been in a state of shock ever since. I just can't seem to find a way to deal with this."

"Jesus, guys!" Blaine responded. "Lighten up. Have another drink. The rest of us don't want to listen to this doomsday crap."

"I do," Tessa interjected.

Blaine gave Tessa a dirty look.

"Oh, fuck you, Blaine," Ruby said. "You're just a drunk. Don't you realize what a momentous year this has been for us? Our friends are disappearing. Here one moment, gone the next."

As he usually did at this point, Fernando sat back in his chair and listened to them bicker. The two of them could argue for hours on end. On occasion, after several margaritas, the argument could get physical. But they always came back the next day in a good mood, ready to drink and argue yet again. Neither of them seemed to take it seriously. The two of them had been best friends/best enemies for years. Fernando couldn't explain it, but he loved listening to them.

"Now that Antonio is gone, I'll have to take over as the enforcer around here," Blaine said finally.

Fernando nodded, because there was an element of truth to what Blaine said. Blaine had helped him on a couple of cases and proved himself quite capable, thanks to his military training, however ancient. And his size made him formidable, even when he wasn't armed.

"Hah! What do you enforce?" Ruby asked.

Blaine raised his margarita. "I enforce the rules and etiquette of this drinking circle. And the first rule is to be here now with whoever's here now. No more of this maudlin talk about who's not here."

Ruby rolled her eyes. "You're a Neanderthal."

"He is! You're right," Tessa added. "I want a divorce."

Fernando laughed. He drained his Modelo and stood to go.

Everyone turned to look at him.

"Cheers!" Fernando said.

Ruby looked worried. "No, don't leave," she pleaded. "I don't want to be left alone with these two cranks!"

Stopping, Fernando bent over and gave Ruby a big hug. Then he turned and walked out of El Farol into the crisp Santa Fe air.

No doubt about it, there was a coolness to the afternoon now, a hint of Fall and the bitter cold to come.

# READERS GUIDE

1. Why is former Santa Fe Police Sergeant Antonio Blake accused of choking Chris Chabot to death during the peyote ceremony in the first chapter? Explain.

2. Who is Doctor Ziggy, the man who runs the peyote circle meeting? What do we learn about him later in the text? What credentials does he possess that enable him to run a therapeutic peyote circle for people who suffer from Post Traumatic Stress Disorder or general anxiety?

3. When former Santa Fe Police Detective Fernando Lopez investigates the peyote circle murder, he interviews the three other patients who were present in the peyote circle that night: Mary Logan, George Boros, and Tom Lujan. What does Lopez learn or infer from their testimony?

4. What eventually happens to Logan, Boros, and Lujan?

5. Who is Joey Alhambra, the man who works for Doctor Ziggy? What is his role at Ziggy's facility in Apache Canyon? What does Lopez discover about him?

6. Who is Sammy Logan? What does Lopez learn from Sammy initially?

7. What is the big break in the case that allows Lopez to identify the person/persons of interest who then become the main suspects? Who provides that information? Explain.

8. What happens when Lopez and Blake finally confront Doctor Ziggy with their suspicions? How does Sammy Logan, of all people, help them?

9. When Doctor Ziggy and Joey Alhambra flee, where do they go? How do Lopez and Blake find out where the two suspects are hiding?

10. What happens when Lopez and Blake corner the two suspects? Who is killed in the shootout that follows?

11. Blake tracks the one suspect who survives the shootout. Where does he find the suspect? When Lopez joins Blake, the two of them make a plan to capture the suspect. What is the plan? Does it work?